Love [illegible]

Worlds Apart

Sunny Randolph set off to find adventure visiting a friend in Kenya, but while she thought she'd packed for everything, there was one unexpected twist she never saw coming.

Martin Karanja had his hands full with the staff and guests of Karanja Safari, so fighting an unexpected attraction to a guest from America was last on his to-do list.

Sometimes, love finds you when you least expect it. And sometimes real love happens. Even worlds apart. Worlds Apart is a contemporary romance novella by eleven-time USA Today bestselling author, Elizabeth Hunter.

Praise for Elizabeth Hunter

Such wonderful and fully developed characters and terrific locations. Elizabeth Hunter is a talented writer who creates wonderful worlds and always tells a story you cannot put down.

SUSAN, GOODREADS.COM REVIEW

The bottom line: if you're not reading Elizabeth Hunter's novels, you should be!

A TALE OF MANY BOOK REVIEWS

Elizabeth Hunter's books are delicious and addicting, like the best kind of chocolate.

THEA HARRISON, NYT BESTSELLING AUTHOR

Worlds Apart

A NOVELLA

ELIZABETH HUNTER

R | P

Worlds Apart
Copyright © 2023 by Elizabeth Hunter
All rights reserved.
ISBN: 978-1-959590-35-4
Paperback edition.

No artificial intelligence was used in the creation of this work of fiction.

No part of this book may be reproduced in any form or by any electronic or mechanical means, including information storage and retrieval systems, without written permission from the author, except for the use of brief quotations in a book review.

Book Cover: Bailey Designs Books
Content Editor: Amy Cissell
Line editor: Anne Victory
Proofreader: Linda, Victory Editing
Formatter: Elizabeth Hunter

First edition 2023

NO AI TRAINING: Without in any way limiting the author's [and publisher's] exclusive rights under copyright, any use of this publication to "train" generative artificial intelligence (AI) technologies to generate text is expressly prohibited. The author reserves all rights to license uses of this work for generative AI training and development of machine learning language models.

For every couple who had to hear:
"This is never going to work."

And to Dawit,
With my whole heart.

Chapter One

Chevy Chase, Maryland

SUNNY SURVEYED the range of clothing laid out across the bed in her old bedroom at her parents' house. "I think I have everything, but I'll need to weigh it to make sure I'm not over my baggage allowance."

"This?" Her mother blinked. "This is all you're taking?"

"The bush plane that goes out to the camp only has so much weight allowed per person for luggage."

"I'm sure this is all very safe but..." Mitsy Cooper Randolph of the Loudon County Coopers considered a trip to Paris to be free-spirited, zesty adventure. "What kind of holiday is this when you're staying in a tent and flying on tiny planes. Is there running water? Hot showers? *A bar?*"

"Yes, obviously. There's all that." She took a deep breath and let it out slowly. "It's going to be great, Mom."

It was going to be great.

Sure, she'd only left the United States twice in her life and both of those trips had been hyper-managed by her mother or her school teachers, but she was turning over a new leaf—and taking some of the holiday time her boss had insisted she use.

She was a new Susannah Randolph, professional single woman and soon-to-be world traveler.

She'd read everything she could on Kenya, the Maasai people, the history and biology of the Mara, and the ecological implications of responsible travel. She'd been keeping track of the camp's blog and followed their social media pages.

She was ready.

Probably.

"How many days will you be gone?" Her mother perched in a wingback chair in a corner of her bedroom, a dry martini in one hand and a small line of confusion resting between her perfectly sculpted eyebrows. "Really, Susannah, what is there to do in *Kenya*?"

"A lot." Sunny tried not to roll her eyes. "Remember Alice Ledama? I'm going to visit her at the safari camp she's managing. I'm going to see lions and elephants and... zebras!" Her eyebrows went up. "Don't you think it's exciting?"

Sunny had checked off everything the safari company and Alice had recommended, long-sleeved shirts in cotton or linen and pants to protect her skin from the sun. A broad sunhat to shade her eyes. Sturdy, broken in hiking boots weren't a problem, since she enjoyed local hikes regularly with her birding club.

"I'm just impressed you're going *anywhere*." Sunny's older sister Lulu appeared from the hallway and leaned against the door jamb. "You never even wanted to go to Europe with me and Mom."

Her older sister looked like a younger clone of her mother, bearing the Cooper blond hair and sky-blue eyes. Sunny got the blue eyes, but she bore a stronger resemblance to her father with her slightly olive skin and dark hair.

"That's because you and Mom go to Europe to shop" —Sunny began to fold her plain cotton underwear and sensible bras so they would fit in the packing cube— "and I don't like shopping."

Lulu sat on the corner of the bed and started to

fold alongside Sunny. “You should bring a bathing suit. Kenya is supposed to have great beaches. And at least one pair of sexy underwear.” She rose and walked to Sunny’s chest of drawers. “What if you meet a hot safari guide or something?”

Mitsy lifted her glass. “Hear, hear. Holiday romances are an experience every young person should have.”

Sunny stifled a laugh. “Mom, Lu, this is *me*. I’m not going to have some wild holiday romance. I couldn’t get a date at the actuarial conference.”

Lulu made a face. “Why would you want to date an actuary?”

“*I’m* an actuary!”

“Exactly.” Lulu pulled out a tiny scrap of lace that pretended to be a bra and tossed it on the bed. “You need someone to liven you up.”

“Susannah, you’ve had all your shots, haven’t you?” Mitsy waved a hand. “Never mind, just drink lots of gin and tonic, darling. It’s medicinal.”

“Not everyone needs a romantic partner.” Sunny glanced at Lulu from the corner of her eye. “I actually *like* being single.”

Mostly. She mostly liked it, except for those times when she didn’t, which were becoming more and more frequent the closer she got to thirty.

It was still a little over a year away, but Sunny had the irritating feeling that she should be...more. That whatever adult benchmarks of success one was supposed to meet by their third decade, she had fallen behind.

Somewhere in the six years since she'd finished college, most of her school friends had drifted into marriage, partnership, or parenting, all while seeming to maintain picture-worthy social lives and brilliant careers.

Everyone she knew seemed to post pictures of holidays Sunny would never brave on her own, so when Alice messaged her about coming to visit the luxury safari camp in the North Mara conservancy, Sunny swallowed her fear of travel, dusted off her passport, threw money at Alice, and bought a ticket to Nairobi.

She could have adventures! She hadn't been the keenest to leave the familiar in the past, but that didn't mean she couldn't branch out and take baby steps out the door.

"Baby steps," she muttered under her breath.

"Baby steps?" Lulu grinned and started rolling Sunny's t-shirts into neat packable tubes. "I wouldn't call going on safari a baby step, little sister. Definitely a big girl step. I'm proud of you."

"Yeah?" Sunny stared at the swiftly disappearing

pile of clothes as she and her sister filed everything into neat packing cubes. "It's going to be great."

"You're going to have an amazing time." Lulu hugged her shoulders. "Alice is going to meet you at the plane, right? The safari plane?"

Sunny nodded, trying not to panic.

"And she gave you detailed directions how to get from the international airport to the local one where the small planes take off?"

"Yes." She gulped. "And I already checked with my phone company and my phone will work as soon as I get there so I can call her if anything goes wrong."

"Then there's nothing to worry about." Lulu grabbed her by the shoulders. "Relax. Your flight is early tomorrow, right?"

Sunny nodded. That was why she'd brought all her clothes to her parents to wash and pack. Her Arlington apartment might have been closer to the airport than her parents' house, but their driver could take her to the airport in the morning and she wouldn't have to leave a car there or battle through public transportation with luggage.

She had her passport, her visa, her vaccination card, her Swahili phrase book, and all her receipts.

"Oh!" Lulu pulled a pair of rose-colored lace panties from her drawer. "These are cute. Take these."

And sexy underwear. She had sexy underwear too.

•◘•◘•◘•◘•

Mara North, Kenya

"MARTIN!"

Martin Karanja had been trying to enjoy his first hot shower in two days. *If another baboon broke into the kitchen...* "What is it?"

His business partner Errol Carberry spoke through the canvas tent wall. "It's the water tank."

He could feel the moment the heated water in his bucket began to cool. He rinsed the soap off his face, quickly washed the rest from his body, and reached for a towel as he shut the overhead shower off. "What's wrong with the tank? Leak?" He doubted it was a leak. Errol was a skilled welder; he wouldn't bother Martin with a leak.

Errol was still on the outside, speaking through the canvas. "The tank is low again, and it shouldn't be based on how many people are in the camp."

"Damn." Martin thought about the group they had flying in the next day. A friend of Alice's, a family from the UK, and one of his favorite guests, Ethel Merriman, a New York octogenarian who celebrated every other birthday in the Mara. Not the biggest group for a week, but they were all going to need water.

"You think it's the elephants again?"

"Possible," Errol said. "The south watering hole is dry right now. They're looking for water, especially with that new baby in the herd. Can I come in?"

"Fine." So much for a quiet morning and tea with his paperwork. "Make yourself at home." He hung his cotton towel to dry on the handmade rack that equipped every tent in the camp. "Start the kettle, will you? I'm just getting dressed."

"Sorry to bother you so early." Errol teased him. "I don't suppose I'm interrupting anything."

Martin shook his head. "This is me, Carberry, not you." He quickly smoothed lotion over his dark brown skin since the air in the Mara was so dry. "Did the South African girl head home already?"

"Last week, Karanja. Keep up."

That was nearly impossible with Errol. Luckily, the man was devoted to work far more than any passing relationship.

"Take a truck out with a crew and see if you can find the leak," Martin said. "I'll talk to Alice about getting a water truck from the village as a backup."

"Right," Errol said. "Six flying in tomorrow?"

"Yes." He reached for the white polo with the *Karanja Safari Camp* logo on the pocket. "It's Ethel's year again."

"Is it?" Errol's voice came from the living area. "I missed the old girl. Which birthday is it now?"

Martin pulled on a pair of khaki cargo pants and walked from the bathing area into the living room. "Eighty-seven this year." He smiled. "This will be her third safari with us."

Errol was standing at the electric kettle, dropping two teabags into Karanja Safari mugs. "She still a fire-cracker?"

Errol Carberry watched the kettle with a devotion inherited from his British forebears. He was third generation British Kenyan and as devoted to the land and the tourism industry as Martin was. Unlike Martin, he was regularly unshaven, averse to any life outside of the camp, and more willing to speak to a hungry lioness than a banker.

Martin sat in a chair next to his desk and reached for the basket of socks he'd tucked underneath. "According to Alice, Ethel asked that we pair her with a different guide this year because the first two were too cautious."

Errol looked up with wide eyes. "Didn't she ride with Kapen last trip?"

"Yes, and he says he won't guide her again. She tried to climb down the riverbank last time to get a better picture of the hippos."

Errol let out a long breath and poured boiling water over the tea. "God save us from Ethel." He looked around Martin's tent. "Why do you have the coolest tent in the camp?"

"Because it's *mine*."

"Mine too," Errol muttered. "At least thirty percent of it is." He took the two cups of tea and handed one to Martin before it could finish steeping.

Martin pulled on socks and reached for the mug. "I'm also the one who has to meet with investors, officials, and bankers when they come for their free stay in the Mara."

"Never mind, you can have the big tent."

Because of his role as the majority owner and public face of Karanja Safaris, Martin's tent was far more than the typical staff housing at the camp.

Most employee tents consisted of a bedroom tent, a shared bathroom, and a shared living space. Martin's sprawling compound had an office, a meeting room with a large dining table, and two bedrooms with private baths. There was a raised wooden porch outside that overlooked the western horizon for the best sunset viewing and a clear window over his bed so he could see the stars.

It paid to be the boss.

He'd offered to let Errol have the other bedroom, but his partner preferred life a little more rugged with lots of privacy for the occasional dalliance with an attractive female guest or passing biologist. He'd built himself a small house next to the water tower on a temporary platform that lifted it into the trees. It was primitive, but it felt like an upgraded treehouse and had the best views of the sunset.

By agreement with their Maasai landlords, no permanent structures could be built anywhere on the property, except those necessary for maintaining equipment. No houses, offices, or bungalows allowed. It was a safari camp without fences or barriers to the wild.

Which in lion country meant they also employed a lot of armed guards.

"So if Ethel isn't content with Kapen" —Errol sipped his tea— "then who are we sending her with? He's our best spotter."

"I thought I could try asking Mingati."

Errol raised an eyebrow. "Why?"

"He likes me."

"Just because he's slightly less of an arse to you doesn't mean that he likes you."

"He's not an arse if you don't force him to be friendly." Martin's Maasai wasn't nearly as good as Errol's, but Mingati spoke fluent Swahili as well as Maasai. The old man refused to speak English—though he understood every word—and wasn't the most friendly wildlife spotter in the area, so he didn't work much.

He was grumpy, anti-social, and able to track a leopard at noon.

Martin shrugged. "You can't deny that he knows the country."

"Mingati is the best spotter I've ever met, but he's a nightmare with guests," Errol said. "He spat on that woman from France, remember?"

"He said it was an accident."

"It wasn't an accident!"

"She kind of deserved it though." Martin cocked his head. "Didn't she?"

"Yes, but it doesn't matter how satisfying it was, none of our guides will work with him now. Ethel will have to live with Kapen."

Martin thought about Ethel Merriman, surly Maasai game spotters, and the paperwork he was supposed to catch up on that week. "You know what? I don't have anyone coming in from the city this week, and you're going to be busy trying to fix that elephant damage to the pipes."

Errol pouted. "It might not be elephants."

"It's always the elephants." Martin slid on a pair of boots. "Why don't I drive the group this week?"

"Are you sure you remember which way to go?"

"Yes, very amusing." Martin added sugar to his tea before he drank it. "The land hasn't changed, Carberry. I still know my way around."

A friend of his manager's, a family of four, and one sprightly retiree.

How much work could they be?

Chapter Two

"WELCOME TO KENYA." The friendly woman at immigration stamped her passport. "I hope you enjoy your holiday."

"Thank you."

Alice called almost as soon as Sunny walked from immigration to the luggage claim, squealing her excitement over the phone.

"How are you feeling?" her friend asked. "Are you exhausted?"

"No, actually." Sunny was a little shocked, but she wasn't that tired. "I had an empty seat next to me on the flight and I slept really well." The cool, dry air of Nairobi was already flowing into the luggage claim. It felt amazing after the humid heat of DC.

"Excellent," Alice continued. "I've arranged a

driver for you; he's a friend of mine. His name is Trevor. He's a really tall guy and he'll probably be wearing shiny mirrored glasses."

Sunny cast her eyes toward the exit where a dozen tall men wearing various mirrored sunglasses waited, most of them looking at their mobile phones. "You may need to be a little more specific."

"I told him to make a sign! Send me a text when you meet him, okay? He'll get you to Wilson and get you through all the traffic. Ah! I cannot believe I'm going to see you soon. Text me when you're at Wilson."

Wilson Airport was the smaller, local airport Sunny would take to get to the Mara North Reserve, the private land trust where Alice worked.

She spotted her bag on the luggage carousel and grabbed it, slinging her backpack over her shoulder and walking toward the crowd of drivers, all of whom came to attention as passengers started to exit.

"Miss, do you need a hotel?"

"I can recommend city tours. My car is available for hire—"

"I have the best rates in Nairobi, madam. Can I recommend—?"

"Sunny!"

She swung her head toward the voice saying her name.

"Sunny Randolph?"

She spotted a tall man with short twisted hair wearing mirrored blue sunglasses waving at her from the back of the crowd.

"Hi!" She waved back. "Trevor?"

"Nice to meet you. Alice sent me." He reached out his hand, guided her through the crowd, and took her suitcase handle. "Wow, so crowded today. Let me help. Are you very tired?"

"Not bad."

"That's great! It's a long flight from Washington, I know." He smiled broadly. "I'm Trevor. Welcome to Nairobi."

•◘•◘•◘•◘•

THE PILOT'S calm voice crackled through the speaker of the small propeller plane, her crisp Indian accent narrating their descent. "And for those departing at the Mara North airstrip, this is our last stop before returning to Nairobi." The plane circled around a dusty dirt track cleared from the grassy savannah.

They leveled out and bounced across the dirt airstrip, kicking up dust as half a dozen trucks and land cruisers began to follow the dirt road running parallel to the plane. Along the edge of the cleared area, there was a tall stand of trees and Sunny did a double take as she realized that the tall things moving at the edge of the trees weren't more trees, but a small herd of giraffes.

Wow.

"Those are giraffes." She blinked, but they were still there.

Wow!

"Welcome to the Mara," the pilot said again. "We hope you enjoy your stay."

Sunny was frozen, watching the herd of giraffes through her small window, until the pilot called out. "You know, there's more if you get off the plane."

She blinked and turned away from the window. "Right." She felt her face warming. "Sorry."

The woman smiled. "Have a great time. Your first visit to Kenya?"

Sunny swallowed her nerves. "First visit anywhere."

"Fantastic!" The woman's eyes lit up. "You came to the best place."

Sunny grabbed her backpack and bent over as she

exited the plane, her eyes immediately met by the glaring Mara sunshine.

"Sunny!"

She squinted and turned to Alice's familiar voice, spotting her friend near a large safari-style truck.

"Alice!" She ran toward her, then stopped. "My bag!"

The man with Alice waved a hand. "I'll get it."

Alice enveloped Sunny in a massive hug. "I can't believe you're really here! When I invited you, I never thought you'd come."

Sunny laughed a little. "I'm kind of shocked myself."

"No." Alice took her by the shoulders and shook her a little. "This is excellent. You have an adventurous spirit; it's time that you came out of your shell."

"Okay." She let out a quick breath and looked up at the massive off-road vehicle they were standing by. "So how do I climb into this thing?"

•◘•◘•◘•◘•

SUNNY'S CAMERA never left her face the entire way to the camp. Herds of zebras and gazelles lined both sides of the dirt road. The driver, John, stopped dead when she squealed from the backseat of the Land Cruiser.

"That's an elephant!" There was an elephant rubbing its side on a tree and shaking the canopy with its scratches. "Oh my god, Alice, that's an elephant!"

Alice laughed. "Yes, you'll see a lot of those."

The Land Cruiser started again, and Sunny decided then and there that she wasn't going to be embarrassed by any of her reactions on this trip.

She'd seen an elephant. That was amazing! Her mind drifted to the percentage of people in the world who had seen a living elephant in the wild. It couldn't have been that large.

"The Mara North is a private conservation project," Alice was telling her about the camp. "The Maasai landowners in the area pooled their property together and manage their grazing along the edges of the park, leaving the majority of the land wild habitat."

"So the park is owned by the local people?"

"Yes, and the safari camps pay them rent to use the land. They can't own it or build permanently, but you're going to see. The camp is so luxurious. It's like a dream."

Sunny smiled. "Aren't you the one who teased me in college about camping for vacation?"

"I will never understand Americans leaving

perfectly nice houses and hotels to exist unbathed in the woods for weeks on end and sleep on the ground." Alice closed her eyes and shook her head. "I like my tent with a full size bed and a bathroom, please. The owner of the camp is the son of a very prominent hotel owner. He knows how to make camping tolerable."

Sunny leaned back, closed her eyes, and breathed in the fresh air and the sunshine. "Alice, this is heaven."

"It's the closest you're going to get on earth." She patted Sunny's knee. "I can't wait for you to meet everyone."

•◘•◘•◘•◘•

MARTIN'S IPAD WAS MISSING. Again.

"Dammit, Alice." He regularly let the camp manager use the iPad when she needed to make a quick change to the schedule. Since they were all linked through his main account, it made the most sense.

The problem was, Alice wasn't the best at putting things back where she found them.

Martin was in the large reception tent where the group visiting area, the fire pit, and the bar were all located. He walked behind the bar and looked through the shelves and drawers.

"Alice, where did you put it?"

They had guests coming and he wanted to be out of the way before the chaos of new people complicated the search. He couldn't call her, she was already on her way to the airport to pick up her school friend.

"Hello?"

Martin popped his head over the bar and saw a dark-haired woman spinning in circles, taking it all in. "Hello."

She turned toward him and raised her sunglasses. "Oh. Hi. Alice said there was a bar, I didn't realize it was right here. She said I could wait here while they got my luggage sorted out, but I didn't know anyone would be around." She pushed her hand forward. "Sorry, I'm Sunny. I don't travel much."

Martin smiled and shook her hand. "I'm Martin. You must be—"

"Is it too early to get a gin and tonic?"

He put a hand on his chest. "Actually I don't—"

"My mother said they're medicinal." She smiled and it transformed her face. "Pretty sure she's just saying that though. She drinks a lot of them when she's golfing."

The smile struck Martin dumb for a moment. The way that a simple expression could transform a pleasant looking woman into someone... incandescent.

He reached for a glass. "Any preference on gin?"

"Oh no, I'm not picky." Her eyes were wide and blue as the sky. Her neck had to be sore from the way she was swinging her head around, trying to take everything in.

Martin decided to tease her a little. "So do you come to this bar often?"

The woman burst into a nervous laugh. "I can't believe I'm here. This is like... I don't know, a movie or something. I didn't know places like this really existed."

"You mean the camp?" He worked hard to make sure his "safari camp" was nothing close to rugged. Coming from a high-end hotel background, he wanted guests to sleep in luxury while they explored the outdoors and experienced the Mara. "Or the countryside?"

"The camp, the country, everything." She looked out the open side of the reception tent, which was a broad shade cover on a raised platform that overlooked the savannah. "I'm drinking at a bar and there are zebras grazing." She pointed over her shoulder. "Like... right there."

Martin smiled. "Welcome to the Mara." He poured two fingers of gin, squeezed a lime over the ice, and filled the rest of the glass with tonic water. "Your gin and tonic, miss."

"Thanks." She gave him that smile again. "The trip from the air strip was the most beautiful drive I've ever taken in my life."

Martin remembered the first time he came to this place, twelve years old and finally old enough to travel with his father for work. His father had never been content with the leased cooperative idea that the Maasai were developing. If John Karanja built a hotel, he wanted to own the land it sat on.

"I was twelve the first time I visited this place," he said. "I still remember how awe-struck I was."

"Where are you from?"

"Nairobi," he said. "City boy. You?"

"Same. Well, city *girl*. I grew up in the Washington, DC area."

"Is your father in government?"

"Oh no, thank God. He's... He works in banking. Kind of boring."

"Ah." Martin leaned on the bar and watched her. "Do you work in banking as well? You're Alice's friend, correct?"

"I am. And yes, kind of. I don't work for the same bank as my dad, but I'm an actuary and I work for an investment fund. I analyze data and numbers to quantify the risk potential for different businesses."

"That sounds interesting."

"It's not." Her smile turned nervous again. "I mean, it's interesting to me, but usually when I describe what I do, I notice people's eyes glazing over." She sipped her gin and tonic. "Most people don't like numbers that much."

"Do you like them?"

She blinked. "I don't think anyone has ever asked me that before."

"If you like your job?"

"No, if I like numbers." The smile began to creep out again. "I like my job as much as I like any job, but I really like numbers."

"Why?"

She relaxed onto the stool and let out a thoughtful sigh. "They're beautiful and elegant. They're like this beautiful language that you don't have to speak aloud."

Her cheeks reddened a little bit and Martin felt a punch of satisfaction. He liked making this woman blush. He liked seeing her smile. He liked her laugh and he really wanted to see her long hair down. It was braided sensibly down her back, but wild feathers of it had pulled away from the braid, probably from the wind.

"And they're easy to understand." She was still talking about numbers. "People can be really..."

Attractive. Intriguing. Unexpected.

"Complicated?" He poured himself two fingers of scotch and mixed a little water in.

"Tiring." There were the red cheeks again. "Not you. You're a lifesaver. But sometimes I'll be talking to someone—and I am terrible about remembering faces and names—so I'll be talking with someone at one of my parents' parties or something and I'll think they're one person but they're really another person and then I'll say something completely inappropriate and make a fool of myself."

"I doubt that."

"No, trust me. I can be really awkward." She nodded and finished her drink. "My sister is brilliant with people. So...confident. And I don't have any reason *not* to be confident, but I still struggle with it. I think it drives my mother crazy, but I don't know how to turn that anxiety off." She blinked. "I can't believe I'm telling you all of this. I guess what they say about bartenders being therapists is true, huh? You probably hear the most private things from the guests here, don't you?"

"Actually, I'm not usually—"

"Sunny?" Alice called from the pathway. "Oh, you met Martin already. Wonderful." She jogged over and put her arm around her friend. “Sunny, this is my boss, Martin Karanja.”

Sunny’s eyes went wide. “Martin... Karanja? As in Karanja Safaris?”

“Of course! My boss. Martin, this is Sunny.” She frowned. “And what are you doing here? I thought you were working on payroll this afternoon.”

“I’m looking for my iPad.”

Sunny was blinking and her cheeks were red again, but this time there was no smile accompanying the flush.

“I left your iPad in the office,” Alice said. “Did you look under the payroll folder? I put both of them right on the top of your desk.”

Martin kept glancing at Sunny, whose expression was frozen. “I didn’t lift up the payroll folder, no. It was probably under there.”

Alice rolled her eyes. “Men are all the same. How you find your own shoes in the morning is a miracle.” She tugged on Sunny’s arm. “Bring your drink along. I want to show you your tent. We’re not booked up this week, so I gave you one of the Duma tents; it has the best view.”

“Oh, I’m...” Sunny quickly swallowed the last of her gin and tonic, then she set her glass down. “I’m done.” She sounded as if she had something in her mouth. "Sorry." She carefully took the slice of lime out and put it in the empty glass. "Sorry." There was a furtive glance at Martin, then she looked away. "Thank you so much for the drink."

"Any time." Martin watched them walk away, Alice's arm firmly around her friend's shoulders. He was hoping he might catch a whisper of their conversation, but the wind stole their words away.

Chapter Three

IT WAS seven in the morning and the sun was up, which meant Sunny could walk to the reception area without an armed guard. The lecture from Alice had been stern the night before. This was an open camp, which meant that anything from elephants to jackals to leopards could wander freely. She was not to leave her tent after dark without waving down a guard with her flashlight.

She slid on her hiking boots after checking for unexpected critters and unzipped the tall tent flap that was her front door for the next week.

The tent itself was a slice of five-star luxury in the middle of the wilderness. There was an elaborately carved wooden bed with a feather topper and soft-as-silk cotton sheets. The bathroom sported a clawfoot tub and shower that overlooked a nearby stream where water trickled softly beneath greenery. Soft woolen rugs were scattered over the floors and plush robes and house slippers were waiting for her.

She and Alice had opened a bottle of wine the night before and watched the sun set in the most brilliant display Sunny had ever seen.

When she stepped onto her small porch, there was an insulated thermos cup full of black tea, as she'd requested, and a covered plate of pastries.

She grabbed a croissant and the tea as she walked toward the reception tent, which was the heart of the safari camp and the gathering place for all the guests for meals and game rides.

"Good morning, Sunny." John, the driver from the day before, waved from beside the Land Cruiser where he was talking with another driver.

"Morning." Sunny waved at him. John was friendly and so far, Sunny hadn't embarrassed herself in front of him like she had with Alice's boss the day before.

Martin Karanja hadn't joined them for dinner the night before. Alice told her she was overreacting, but Sunny wanted to die when she realized that the man she'd so boldly asked to fix her a gin and tonic was the owner of the entire operation.

Typical! Go to a new country and mistake the owner of the camp for a bartender. Well done, Sunny.

He must have thought she was so rude.

"How did you sleep?"

She started when she heard Martin's voice from over her shoulder. "Hi."

"Good morning." His smile was wide and teasing. "Were you comfortable sleeping with the zebras?"

"I decided to sleep in the tent." Sunny pointed over her shoulder. "Sleeping *with* the zebras seemed a little risky after the whole hyena lecture that Alice gave me last night."

Wait, was she flirting with him? What was her mouth doing?

What are you doing Sunny???

Martin smiled. "Probably a good plan."

Sunny was going to blame his smile, which was handsome, wide, and disarming. It would be strange *not* to flirt when in the presence of that smile.

"I'm sorry I thought you were a bartender," she blurted.

There she was. Back in awkward form.

Martin frowned. "Are you saying my gin and tonic wasn't professional?"

"What?" She blinked. "No! I just—"

"Please." He lifted a hand and laughed a little. "I

was not offended at all. And I'm glad my cocktail skills have not diminished."

"Everything is amazing." She looked around. "The views. The food. The rooms—*tents*." She lifted her cup. "Even the tea is good. And I get my own mug."

"We don't use any single use plastics here in the camp. They're illegal in Kenya, unless you have health reasons to use them."

"So you're saying I'm not special because I got a mug with my name on it?" She held up the mug with Sunny written in bright gold marker.

He smiled and looked away. "I suspect you're special for entirely different reasons."

Okay, she didn't know what to say to that. Probably Martin was charming with all the guests, especially single female ones. According to Alice, Sunny was expressly forbidden from falling for Martin's partner Errol, because he was... Well, Alice had a few choice phrases, one of which might have rhymed with *tan glut*. But she hadn't mentioned anything about her boss.

"Right. Um..." Sunny started walking toward the reception tent again, only to run into Martin's shoulder as he headed toward the Land Cruisers. "Sorry."

"No, it's my fault. I should have been looking..." He cleared his throat. "Did you get some breakfast?"

She held up the croissant. "Just this."

"If that's enough to hold you for an hour or so, I believe the chef has packed a proper breakfast for us to eat near the river this morning."

"Oh that sounds..." She blinked. "Did you say *us*?"

"Yes." His smile was back. "By special request, I will be driving your group this week. It should be fun. It's been years since I was behind the wheel for a whole week."

"Special request?" She looked around. "Who...?" If Alice got even a hint that she was interested in Martin, she'd start playing matchmaker hard. "Did Alice suggest that?"

"Oh no." Martin started back on the path toward the trucks, but he pointed in the distance. "Head to reception. I can't wait for you to meet Ethel."

•◘•◘•◘•◘•

"SO I TOLD the young man steering the boat to follow that thing, will you?" The women with the silver pixie-cut gesticulated wildly. "But he wouldn't! Said it was an arapaima and it was dangerous. I didn't see how it could be that dangerous. We were on a boat after all. But he was a skittish one."

Sunny hadn't blinked in fifteen minutes. Ethel Merriman hadn't stopped regaling the group with tales from her many adventures since Sunny arrived at the reception tent. The Calaways from Arizona and their two adolescent boys rounded out Sunny and Ethel's group.

One of the Calaway boys asked Ethel, "Did you catch any fish?"

"I'm not a game fisherman, son. But I'll catch my dinner if I need to."

"Were there piranhas in the river?" the other boy asked.

"Many of them, but they're not as dangerous as the movies say. The real danger in the river is the candiru. Now that's one you boys would need to watch for if you visit the Amazon because the candiru will sense if someone is peeing in the water and then they'll swim right up—"

"Okay!" Alice clapped her hands beside Ethel to stop that train from leaving the station. "Who's ready for a game drive?"

Everyone stood, including Ethel, who barely came up to Sunny's shoulder. The boys ran to the car with their parents following them, leaving Ethel and Sunny on the deck.

"I guess the two single gals should stick together," Ethel said to Sunny. "Is this your first trip to Kenya?"

"Yes." She held her hand out as Ethel started down the steps. "My first real trip anywhere. I mean, I've been to Paris once and to Athens for a school trip because my parents kind of insisted, but I don't travel much for work."

"I didn't either," Ethel made it down the steps, steadying herself on Sunny's arm. "Not until I retired. Now I spend every other birthday here, and in the other years, I go someplace new. Next year I've got a trip planned to Papua New Guinea."

"Wow. How old are you?" Sunny wanted to bite her tongue. "I'm so sorry, that's none of my business."

"I don't mind telling you! I'm eighty-seven this year. Proud of every year."

"Wow." Sunny would have guessed late seventies at the latest. "So what's the secret to living a long life?"

"That's easy," Ethel said. "Just don't stop."

•◘•◘•◘•◘•

MARTIN DROVE the Land Cruiser to a curve of the river where staff from the camp hopped out and quickly set up a folding table and the omelets the chef had prepared for the guests, along with fresh fruit, mango juice, and warm rolls baked that morning.

He was waiting by the truck when Alice walked over.

"Why are you sitting by the truck like a lump, eh? Go and join your guests."

He glanced at Ethel, Sunny, and the American family. "Guides and spotters usually eat on their own. I don't want to intrude."

"I'm going to join them too. You're the owner of the camp, Martin. You want to take all your meals this week with Mingati?"

Martin glanced over his shoulder where the surly game spotter was crouched on the grass, leaning against a tire and silently drinking cornmeal porridge and sweet milk tea. He squinted into the distance, ignoring both Alice and Martin both.

"Fair point." Martin decided that eating with the guests wouldn't be too unprofessional, especially if Alice was joining him. "Your friend is having a good time?"

Alice nudged his side. "I told you she was beautiful."

"I'm not... That's hardly the point, Alice. I'm simply asking if she's feeling welcome at the camp."

"Sunny is the type to be happy anywhere. She's very content, but not very good at standing up for herself sometimes."

"Ah. She seemed a bit nervous yesterday."

"Hmm." Alice shrugged. "That can happen when she's around men she thinks are attractive."

Martin blinked and Alice continued to the riverside to sit next to Ethel, leaving the seat near Sunny the only open one at the breakfast table. He hesitated for a moment.

What was Alice doing? Was she trying to tempt him into a holiday romance with her friend? That wasn't something he did.

Martin had been raised to be professional with guests at all times. His father was always quick to remind him that someone paying you for the use of a room was not a friend and couldn't be. They were a customer and one always had to keep the rules of proprietorship at the front of one's mind.

She wasn't a woman he could flirt with; she was a guest.

Then Sunny looked over her shoulder, squinted into the sunlight, and smiled.

Damn that smile.

Martin walked to the edge of the river where the folding tables had been covered with fresh white linens, heaping plates of fruit, and steaming omelets prepared at the camp kitchen for the guests.

They were seated on the edge of a riverbank and in the distance, hippos and crocodiles sunned themselves in the silt-filled river. A herd of zebras was grazing nearby, and two curious vervets perched in an acacia tree. Birdsong filled the air, and in the river, hippos snorted as they floated in the muddy shallows.

"Hello." Sunny motioned to the seat beside her. "Would you care to join us? There's plenty of food."

"Thank you." Martin quickly took his seat and glanced down the table. "Alice mentioned that you wouldn't be averse to my company, so I thought I would join you."

Both the American parents and Ethel were quick to agree.

"Please!"

"Make yourself at home."

"Wait, is this where you live all the time?" the older boy asked. "Do you live your whole life at the safari camp?"

His brother piped up. "I want to live in a tent all the time too."

Martin smiled as he helped himself to a mushroom omelet; he could tell the entire table was curious. "I don't live here all the time. We have an off season here in the Mara, and during that time I have a house in Nairobi where I live."

Mrs. Calloway said, "Nairobi is the big city we flew into, boys."

"Ohhhh."

Martin took a glass of juice that Sunny held out to him. "Thank you."

"You're welcome." She looked around the table. "It seems like such a small group this week."

"It's hard to predict how many people will come from week to week. Some are booked out months in advance and some will fly in at the last minute if we have space. But it's early in the season. The wildebeest have just started their migration, so most visitors will wait until they are really moving."

"Alice said this time was the best to come though."

Martin nodded. "It is. It's early so there won't be much crowding if you want to go to the national park. The weather is beautiful and cool. She advised you well."

While Martin finished his omelet, Sunny turned her attention to a story that Ethel was sharing with the table, an amusing anecdote from a few years ago when she nearly fell out of the Land Cruiser in the middle of a wildebeest stampede.

"I told Kapen that he needed to drive *into* the skid, but he wasn't very keen on advice from an old lady."

Alice's eyes were wide with alarm. "Mrs. Merriman, you have to promise me that you will not try to climb on top of the Land Cruiser when Martin is driving."

Sunny leaned over to him. "Alice says Ethel comes here every few years."

Martin enjoyed the fresh smell of lemon and flowers that scented her dark hair. "She spends her birthday here every other year. Amazingly, our insurance hasn't discovered her antics. If they had, I imagine our premiums would increase with alarming swiftness."

"So is the new guide..." She looked over toward the truck. "I forgot his name."

"Mingati isn't a guide, he's a wildlife spotter. It's a unique talent and he's very good, but he can be very...

Surly.

Impatient.

Spitting?

Sunny was slightly more kind. "He seems like a very internal person."

"You're very kind, Miss Randolph." He smiled and reached for a bowl of cut fruit. "Mingati is excellent at what he does, but most of the guides don't like working with him. With his talent for knowing where the big cats are, I thought he might be able to help me keep Ethel in check. She's easily distracted by shiny objects and cheetahs."

"Aren't we all?"

Martin glanced to the side and saw her smiling again. "I confess, sometimes I need to be reminded of this place and how unique it is. I suppose we can lose appreciation for the beauty right in front of us when we see it every day."

She opened her mouth, then closed it. "I suppose you're right. But maybe if you recognize that, you're not as likely to take it for granted."

He smiled. "Miss Randolph, I think you are very wise."

Her cheeks flushed again. "Please call me Sunny. Miss Randolph sounds so formal."

"Only if you call me Martin." He finished his fruit and juice, then he stood when he sensed the meal was winding down. "If everyone is finished, we can continue with our morning game drive. I hope your cameras are ready."

Chapter Four

SUNNY LET the warm water pour over her face, reveling in the scent of lemon-scented soap and warm water cascading over her sore body. She'd already washed her hair and cleaned off the sweat and dust accumulated during two game rides, a fishing trip to the river with the boys, and a rousing game of charades before dinner. Now she was enjoying the comforts of her luxurious safari tent while the rest of the camp enjoyed after-dinner drinks in the reception tent.

Her first full day on safari had been everything she was hoping for and more. Her camera had been glued to her face all day, taking in the herds of antelope, the grazing buffalo, and the slowly moving elephants that Martin spoke to as if they were annoying neighbors.

The roads through the park were nothing more

than dirt tracks that led through the most stunning landscape Sunny had ever seen in her life. They'd passed through no towns or settlements in their hours of driving, and most of the day, it felt as if they were the only people on the face of the earth.

Flocks of birds dancing overhead. Endless crowds of zebras and the ever-present clutches of giraffes nibbling the trees. They had driven near one group with a few new calves and watched as the ungainly babies cocked their head at the passing trucks, twitched their huge ears, then galloped away with their elders.

The most stunning nature documentary on earth couldn't hold a candle to the real thing.

Sunny wrapped her hair in a towel and wrapped another large bath sheet around her body, the cool air a relief after the dust of the day. While the rest of the camp had continued visiting long after dinner, Sunny was tapped out and overwhelmed by socializing.

In her everyday life, she interacted with very few people. Her job was solitary and most of her reports were written and transmitted by email or—rarely—given over teleconference. She waved at the security guards in her building, knew the names of the local Indian restaurant staff by their voices, and spoke with her boss weekly.

Being surrounded by social animals felt far more foreign than communing with giraffes.

Sunny slid her feet into her slippers, grabbed her flashlight, and walked toward the tent flap that opened to the savannah. Wary of all the warnings about wandering at night, she unzipped the doorway, quickly re-zipped the netting to prevent bugs from flying in, then sat in the canvas chairs on her small porch, watching the dance of stars in the East African sky.

The sun had gone down and shimmering midnight blue lingered on the horizon. Overhead, the sky was packed with so many celestial lights that Sunny could barely take it in. She leaned forward, looking for the moon, and her flashlight tumbled from her lap.

She picked it up and set the light down on her small table but stood when she heard rustling in the brush.

She grabbed the flashlight and shone it into the darkness. "Whatever is out there," she spoke into the darkness. "I'm going right back inside and—"

"Sunny?"

She let out a relieved breath and closed her eyes. "Martin?"

"Yes, it's me." He stepped closer on the rock-lined path that cut through the grass. "Could you...?"

"Oh!" She lowered the flashlight. "Sorry."

He caught sight of her, blinked, and dropped the beam of his flashlight to the ground. "I'm sorry, I saw your flashlight waving and thought you needed an escort to the reception tent. I didn't mean to interrupt your bath."

Sunny glanced and down and realized that she was still in her towel and hair turban.

Kill me. Let me die now.

"Right." Her voice squeaked. "Sorry. I, uh, came out to look at the stars, but I dropped my flashlight and I didn't mean to signal anyone..." She blinked. "Is that a machine gun?"

He looked at the firearm slung over his shoulder. "Uh... no. Yes. It's a rifle not a machine gun."

"Why...?" She blinked. "Lions."

He nodded. "Lions."

Okay, so that was a thing that was different.

"I wasn't waving for an escort, I just dropped my flashlight but thank you. That was very thoughtful." *And I am still standing in my towel.*

Martin stepped closer. "No, I shouldn't have assumed."

Sunny opened her mouth, closed it, then said, "But you're responsible for keeping the lions away so...you probably should."

Martin gestured over his shoulder. "There is a local

pride just over the nearest ridge. They are hunting right now, so you might hear them."

Sunny didn't even have the words to respond to that. She was still in her towel and goosebumps were rising on her skin. They might have been from the breeze, the idea of hunting lions, or just maybe the idea of Martin Karanja seeing her in next to nothing.

"So." She cleared her throat. "Is everyone still up at the reception tent?"

"The Calloways retired with their two boys, but Ethel will likely be playing backgammon with Alice until midnight."

So they were just pretending that Sunny hanging out naked and wrapped in a towel was nothing remarkable.

"Right. That sounds fun."

"You could join them if you like."

Sunny looked down at her towel. "I think—"

"You could join me." Martin adjusted the strap of his rifle. "For a drink."

Oh!

Oh.

She heard her mother's voice in the back of her mind. *Holiday romances are an experience every young person should have.* This could be it. She could have a story, an adventure. A handsome man asked her for a drink while he protected her from lions.

Kind of.

Sunny smiled. "Just give me a few minutes. I'll put some clothes on."

Martin's smile lit up the night. "Of course."

She was waiting for him to walk away, but he stayed.

Sunny moved to the flap of the tent. "So I'll meet you at the bar?"

"Ah, no." His eyebrows went up and he nodded toward the left. "The lions, remember?"

He still had to escort her with the very large rifle.

"Right." She ducked inside the tent. "The lions."

•◘•◘•◘•◘•

WHAT ARE YOU DOING? *Are you turning into Carberry?*

He was silent as he escorted Sunny to the reception tent where the lights glowed and staff and guests were drinking, playing cards, and exchanging stories about the day.

Don't overreact, Karanja. It was as if he could hear his partner's cocky British accent in his head. *It's just a drink with a woman, not a marriage commitment.*

Sunny walked behind him on the narrow path and he could smell the bright lemon scent of her shampoo in the soft breeze that soughed through the trees.

Talk to her, you idiot.

"How did you enjoy your activities today?" Martin glanced over his shoulder while still sweeping his eyes over the brush to watch for any movement in the grass. "Any notes for your guide?"

"It was amazing. Better than amazing." She fell quiet and he turned just on the edge of the clearing to see her staring at the sky.

"What is it?"

Her eyes were shining when she looked at him. "You get to see this every night. I wonder if you realize how extraordinary it is."

Martin reached out his hand. "I don't make a habit of ignoring the extraordinary."

Her head tilted to the left for a moment, as if she was listening to something in the distance. This time when the smile overtook her face, it was a slow bloom, like a morning glory opening to the sun.

Extraordinary.

HE WAS sleepy when he opened his eyes the next morning but he regretted nothing. Though he and Sunny hadn't been given a moment of privacy the night before, he'd enjoyed seeing her open up with Alice.

They'd played cards late into the night, Alice sharing a simple card game she'd learned in Ethiopia that allowed for conversation and drinks. Ethel had joined them, along with their regular bartender Leboo and Errol. Luckily, his partner was keeping his distance from Sunny, probably because Alice had warned him off.

He rose and walked to the sink to wash his face, examining his unshaven jaw in the mirror. He'd been considering growing out his beard, despite his father's objections. What could the old man say, after all? He was in the Mara for months, perhaps it was the perfect time to try growing a beard.

Sunny's skin looks very smooth.

He shook his head at the thought and laughed at himself. She was an American professional on holiday. No doubt, if romance was on her mind, it would be of the fleeting nature and that wasn't what Martin was looking for.

Even when he was young, he'd been wary of women. Too many lectures from his father about the fortune hunters who might want to ensnare the Karanja heir probably scarred him for life.

It's a pleasant flirtation, nothing more.

Martin picked up his razor and carefully began to soap his jaw.

"It's nothing," he whispered to his reflection. "What can it hurt to enjoy the company of a pleasant woman?"

Sunny Randolph was in Kenya for a week and a half. She would leave his camp in four more days and move on with her life. Until then? Why not enjoy her beautiful smile and pleasant conversation.

What could it hurt?

•◘•◘•◘•◘•

"ETHEL, if you keep trying to crawl to the roof of the truck, I'm going to have to keep stopping and then we're going to miss the leopard Mingati spotted this morning."

The younger Calloway boy piped up from the back seat. "I don't want to miss the leopard!"

Ethel sighed and sat down. "You did this on purpose, Martin."

He started driving again, spotting the smirk on

Mingati's face as he continued across the dirt track that led east to the gorge.

"I don't know what you're talking about, Ethel."

"Putting me with kids. You know I can't stand to disappoint a kid."

Martin smiled. "I cannot think what you mean. Your walking partner is Miss Randolph."

He glanced in the mirror to check on the guests. Sunny and Ethel were in the first row with the open roof over them and the second row where Mr. and Mrs. Calloway sat. Their boys, Austin and Jack, were in the last row of seats, safely restricted from standing in the vehicle.

"Come on, Ethel." Sunny distracted her. "You were telling me last night how hard it was to get a good picture of a leopard. We don't want to miss our chance. Tell me more about living in New York. I've only been to visit a few times."

Sunny was an invaluable partner for Ethel, and she was good natured about the older woman who could be more than a little opinionated.

The herds were moving that morning, and they had to stop multiple times to let animals pass. The wildebeests were still in the national park, so the majority of the traffic consisted of zebras, gazelles, and impalas.

"Hyenas, boss." Mingati muttered in Maasai and gestured to the left. "Big pack with little ones."

Martin responded in English. "If they have cubs, they'll be settled in that area for a while, yes?"

"Oh yeah." Mingati squinted at the horizon. "Just letting you know. We'll catch them on the way back. Ol-keri won't stay in the gorge for long. She'll move on tonight."

Leopards were one of the hardest animals for the spotters to predict. They were solitary, elusive, and masters of camouflage. The spotters could go weeks without seeing one in clear view. The fact that this female was hunting on the edge of the conservancy was a chance Martin didn't want to pass up.

He glanced in the mirror again to see Sunny pointing at something in the distance, smiling and speaking animatedly to Ethel. One of the boys asked her a question and she turned to engage with him before she started talking with Mrs. Calloway about traveling with her children.

She was kind. Sunny was the perfect name for her, because everyone who spoke with her came away smiling.

Mingati muttered something in Maasai that Martin didn't catch. "What was that?"

"Good woman." Mingati switched to Swahili. "Alice's friend. No complaining."

It was the first time Martin had heard Mingati compliment any guest. Ever. "She's a lovely person," he responded in Swahili. "Kind to everyone."

Mingati cut his eyes to the side. "Don't be dumb, boss."

"I don't know what you mean."

"Yeah, you do."

Chapter Five

ALICE LEANED ON THE BAR, whispering to Sunny. "What are you waiting for? You should make a move."

"What?" Sunny heard the squeak in her voice and coughed to clear her throat. "Alice, he's just being nice. I'm sure he's like this with all the guests."

"I'm telling you, he is not. I have managed this camp for over a year now. He is not like this with any of the guests. I mean, he's more personal with Ethel because she's been coming here for years, but usually he says hello, waves from a distance, and spends the rest of his time in his office or on the phone. I am telling you, he is *in to you*."

Sunny felt her face heating, hating for the millionth time how easily she blushed.

Actually, she usually didn't blush very often, but for some reason, this week her cheeks had been on overdrive. Maybe it was the latitude.

"I don't even know what to do." She swallowed the rest of her gin and tonic and held out her glass. "How do you make a move? What does that even mean? Do I just run up and kiss him? People don't do that!"

"I feel like that might get the message across." Alice shrugged. "Why not?"

"Alice!"

"Sunny!" Her friend rolled her eyes and refilled her drink. "You wait for everything in your personal life to happen, and I have never understood why. You're not like this professionally. When you want something or have an opinion, you speak up. You renegotiated your contract six months ago and they gave you more than you were asking."

"That's work." *I know what I'm doing at work.* "I'm just not...." She leaned closer to Alice "I'm not very confident with men. Lulu was always better at flirting and dating and all that. When a boy made friends with me, it was usually because they wanted to get to know my sister."

"That is ridiculous!" Alice laughed. "You are beautiful. Talented and smart. You are easy to talk to and you're interesting. Everyone on staff was shocked when I told them you were single."

"Why were they asking?" Sunny's eyes went wide. "People were asking if I was single?"

"Of course. When they saw how the boss likes you—"

"No! Men don't see me that way. I think you're mistaking politeness with romantic interest. Martin has been nothing but friendly—"

"And that's all he will be unless you let him know that you're interested in him. He is very respectful of boundaries. It took him weeks to call me by my first name when I started here because he was *so* professional."

Sunny took two big gulps of her gin and tonic, feeling the burn on the second gulp. "You put more gin in this one."

"For courage." Alice took her by the shoulders and spun her around. "Martin! You're taking Ethel and Sunny on their night drive tonight, aren't you?"

Sunny felt like dying when she realized the subject of their conversation had been in the mess tent right behind her.

"Hey." She raised a hand and waved weakly.

Martin smiled and it transformed his face from stern to playful in a second. "I was just coming to find you, Miss Randolph. Ethel says she's happy to skip the night drive tonight, but Mingati and I are still here if you'd like to go."

"She would." Alice nudged her forward. "We were just talking about how amazing it is when you put the camera aside and experience the savannah in the dark."

"Absolutely," he said. "It's a tremendous experience. I wouldn't want you to miss it."

"I'd love to..."

Martin cocked his head. Sunny's attention was a little wobbly from two quick cocktails, and he looked as put-together as he had that morning.

"To go. On the night drive, I mean. Even if it's just me." She turned to Alice. "Do you want to go? Can you?" *Please?*

"Of course," Martin said. "Alice is more than welcome to come along."

"No, I can't," Alice said. "Don't be silly. I'll be here when you get back but it's Leboo's night off. I have to make drinks."

"So we'll meet her when we return." Martin smiled. "Ready when you are."

Sunny turned to Alice one more time with panicked eyes.

"Make a move," Alice whispered. "Jumping on

him and kissing him will be fine. I promise he won't object."

"Alice—"

"Have fun!" She grabbed the empty cocktail glass from Sunny's hand. "Don't try to take pictures; you're not a professional with the right lenses, they'll probably all look muddy. Just experience the night." She turned Sunny around and shoved her toward Martin. "Here you go, boss! Have fun."

Sunny nearly fell into Martin's chest. "Hi."

He cocked out his elbow. "May I escort you to the truck, Miss Randolph?"

She couldn't stop her smile or the automatic way her hand went to his angled elbow. "I'd be delighted, Mr. Karanja."

They walked out to the truck and Mingati was already inside. He sent Sunny a head nod, then climbed into the cab. She stepped up and into the first row of the lifted Land Cruiser and took the spot between the driver and the spotter's seat. It was just her, Martin, and Mingati.

They drove off into the night and the whoop of hyenas in the distance told Sunny this was going to be different than the game drives in the morning and afternoon.

Martin drove the truck up the river track and

under the trees along the bank. The lights of the camp fell away, darkness enveloped them, and all she could hear was the sound of the engine and Mingati's low voice directing Martin as he drove.

They stopped in an isolated spot clear of the trees. Sunny could hear the river rushing in the distance and heavy movement in the grass.

"What is that?" she whispered.

Martin turned and kept his voice low. "I'm going to flash the spotlight at the ground around the truck. Keep your eyes on the grass. We don't shine the light directly at the animals, but you'll still be able to see if I shine the light on the ground."

Since the truck was stopped, she stood and stuck her upper body through the cut out in the roof, resting her forearms on the hood of the Land Cruiser.

Martin reached up and flipped on the light, pointing the soft glowing beam at the dusty road. As soon as the light turned on, Sunny looked into the grass and immediately spotted what had been making the noise in the grass.

A group of elephants was standing in the thick grass along the river, moving slowly as they grazed. Juvenile elephants were with them, three of what Martin had called "teenagers," one smaller elephant that was dwarfed by the largest one, and two other large elephants.

"They're so beautiful." It wasn't the first time she'd been treated to the sight of an elephant, but it was the first time she felt as if she reached out, she'd be able to run her hands along their thick, wrinkled skin.

"They're not scared of us?"

Martin laughed a little. "That female is the biggest matriarch on the conservancy."

As if she'd understood him, the large female turned and lifted her trunk at Martin.

"I see you, Kihari. I know it was you girls digging up our pipes again."

Mingati laughed and said something in Maasai.

"I don't think so." Martin turned to Sunny. "The south pond where they usually get their water is dry right now. That's why they've been digging up our pipes at the camp and grazing upriver at night."

"They're beautiful."

"Kihari!" Martin shouted at the elephant again.

She raised her trunk and snorted toward the truck.

"Show Sunny your baby, old mother."

"There's a baby?" Sunny was going to die. The elephants she'd seen so far had mostly been young bulls that wandered around the conservancy on their own. This was the first family group she'd seen up close and she was thrilled to see teenage elephants, much less a baby.

As if the elephants understood Martin, they parted and Sunny caught a peek of a small trunk from underneath one of the smaller females.

"Ohhhh, it's a *baby* baby." She melted as the tiny elephant calf came into view.

Mingati chuckled.

"It's not Kihari's, it's one of her daughter's. Little girl was born earlier this season."

"She's precious." Sunny had never been tempted to jump out of the Land Cruiser like Ethel, but she was in that moment. "How can anything top this?"

Martin caught her eye and smiled. "We'll keep trying but it's hard to compete with a baby elephant."

They watched the family grazing for nearly a half an hour before they carried on.

The night drive was magical, and Sunny didn't even try to take a picture. After a full two hours of driving across the dark plains, Martin drove onto one of the main roads and turned toward lights in the distance.

"We'll drop Mingati at his house before we return to the camp, if that's all right with you." Martin turned and looked at Sunny for approval. "It's on the way."

"I don't mind. He's had a long day showing us

everything." She leaned forward and touched the older man's shoulder. "*Ashe*, Mingati. Did I say that right?"

The old man turned and the corner of his mouth lifted. "You're welcome, Miss Sunny."

Martin turned to look at her but said nothing.

Mingati faced the front again and grunted something at Martin.

"I heard you this afternoon, old man." Martin shook his head a little as the dirt road turns to gravel.

They drove into the small village lined with wooden fences, small shops, and houses set back from the road. It was the first time Sunny had driven through the local village and she craned her neck to take everything in. After a few moments they pulled up to an iron gate that fronted a large house.

Mingati grunted at Martin, threw his red and blue plaid wrap around his shoulder, and climbed out of the truck to walk to a large white-washed house with high windows and a red roof.

"That's Mingati's house?" Sunny blinked.

Martin smiled. "He owns a good portion of the conservancy, so he manages a large herd of cattle and is entitled to a large portion of the lease money. I don't think he has to work at all, but he's the best spotter in the area."

"Wow."

"We'll visit a traditional village with the group, but honestly? This is where most of the Maasai people in the area actually live. Only a few of the older people live in traditional villages anymore."

"Is that a good thing or a bad thing?"

Martin turned again. "Would you like to sit in the front on the way back?"

"Oh, sure. That way you don't have to keep turning around for all my questions." Sunny jumped out of the Land Cruiser and climbed into the passenger's seat. She looked at Martin, now without the barrier of the seat between them. "Hi."

He smiled. "Hello."

They pulled back onto the road and he answered the question she'd posed earlier. "Is it a good thing or a bad thing? I don't know that it is either. It's simply a thing that happens. Are ways of traditional life lost when everyone moves into more modern towns? Of course. But are you going to tell people that they shouldn't want a house with running water and modern kitchens? What can you say? Of course they like those things."

"You're not from the country though, right? You mentioned a house in Nairobi."

"I am a city boy, born and raised." He drove slowly through the town, moving around the occasional cow and more than one dog. "I first came out to the Mara with my father when I was young and I fell in love with this place. I always wanted him to open a hotel here, but he has very decided ideas about ownership. He would never sign a lease for an operation."

"So the safari camp is all you?"

"It is me and it is Errol too. We've been friends since we were boys, and his family kind of cut him off, but that was probably the best thing for him." Martin smiled.

"Wild youth?"

"He was a young man with very little direction. We will leave it at that. But an excellent friend. Always a very loyal friend."

"How about you? Were you wild when you were young?"

Martin raised his eyebrows. "The only son of John Karanja? Oh no, I was not allowed to be wild. My parents weren't as accommodating as Errol's if I misbehaved."

"My parents were pretty strict too. But kind. They just had very...decided ideas about proper behavior, you know?"

"It sounds like our families are maybe very similar." Martin looked at her with a smile. "Did you expect that on the other side of the world?"

Sunny smiled. "I think this trip has taught me that I should always pack sunscreen and never pack expectations."

Martin laughed with his whole chest, and Sunny felt like the most clever woman in the world.

"I have a spot I want to show you," Martin said. "You were enjoying the stars the other night, correct?"

"Yes, but I don't want to take any extra time if you're tired," she said. "You've been driving all day."

"It's no problem for me, unless you want to get back."

Take a chance, Sunny. Make a move.

"I'm good." She took a deep breath. "What did you want to show me?"

Karanja, take it slow.

He was fairly certain that Sunny was interested in him. He'd spent the previous three days watching her around the other guests and employees at the camp. She only seemed to blush around him, and Alice was nearly throwing the woman into his arms.

But he also sensed that she was a little shy. Not with everyone, but perhaps with him. Maybe it was his accent. Maybe it was because he was foreign. Or maybe she was simply shy around men.

Talk to her, you idiot.

They'd been driving to the ridge in silence.

"You seem like someone who has traveled," Martin said. "Is that correct?"

"Me?" Her eyes went wide. "A little, but not much. I've been on a couple school trips, and to Paris and London. That's probably a lot of traveling for most Americans, but most of my friends travel a lot more. Like Alice."

He nodded. "Yes, Alice is definitely a wanderer. I think we were lucky to find her and even more lucky that she agreed to stay put for ten months out of the year."

"I think she agreed to take the job because it pays for those two months of the year when she can travel the world." Sunny smiled. "She came to visit me in DC last year and we had a great time. She's very adventurous."

"And you're not?"

She shook her head. "I enjoy my work, so I don't take much time off."

"You said that you loved mathematics. I remember."

She pursed her lips. "Mathematics."

"What?" He felt like a smile was plastered to his face. Were his cheeks going to stick that way?

"I just think your accent is really cute. I love the way you say mathematics."

"You think *my* accent is cute?" He was fairly certain she was blushing, but it was hard to tell in the dark car. "I think yours is very cute."

"I don't have an accent. My mother does, but she's from Virginia."

"I don't have an accent either, what are you talking about?"

Sunny giggled. "Okay, I see your point."

He turned off the road and began to climb the hill to his favorite stargazing point. "Are there many Kenyans where you live?"

"I don't think so. Lots of African-American people in DC, but I don't know about Kenyans."

"You'd be able to spot us," Martin said. "We're the best dressers."

"Is that so?"

"Undoubtedly, Miss Randolph." He winked at her. "You might need to come back and visit Nairobi so I can take you some place a little more formal than a safari camp."

She was silent. Had he overstepped? Did she consider him forward? He parked the car at the top of the ridge and turned to her. "Sunny—"

"Alice said I should just kiss you," she blurted out.

Martin lost the power of speech.

So... not too forward after all.

He watched her as he opened the truck door and shut it. He kept his eyes on hers as he walked around the hood of the truck, to her door, opened it, and helped her out of the Land Cruiser in silence.

Martin took her hand and led Sunny to the outcropping of rocks that jutted up from the grass on the top of the overlook. Then he turned and pulled her closer.

Her body was pressed against his.

"Look up," he whispered.

She looked up and the stars reflected in her eyes, a million sparks of light that made her mouth open in wonder.

Martin leaned down and pressed his lips to hers.

Her mouth was so small, he smiled.

Sunny blinked. "Martin?"

"Can I tell you a secret?"

"Yes." No hesitation.

"I've never kissed a white woman before."

Her mouth formed a delightful O. "Is it different?"

Martin kissed her again, this time letting his lips linger and explore the curve of her bottom lip, the defined line of her upper lip, the corners that turned up. He nibbled along her bottom lip and she smiled, opening wider and he took her invitation to explore more.

It was different. Kissing Sunny was different on every level.

She was a guest.

She was an American.

She was irresistible.

He pressed her against the side of the Land Cruiser, the warmth of the engine heating the metal against her back. He placed a hand at the back of her neck, stroking the soft skin there. She sighed into his mouth and it was a surrender.

She put her hands on his waist and pulled him closer, pressing their bodies together. He kept his hips tilted away; his body was already reacting to her taste and scent.

"Sunny." He peppered kisses along the line of her jaw. "I don't do this."

"Neither do I." Her hands dug into the small of his back.

He closed his eyes and pressed his cheek to hers. "Is this a bad idea?"

Sunny pressed her palm to his other cheek and whispered, "If it is, I don't care."

Chapter Six

THE LAST TWO days of Sunny's holiday in the Mara passed in a whirlwind of fun, game drives, a trip to the national park and the wildebeest migration that made Sunny feel like she might never feel fly-free again.

She was still picking leaves from her shirt when Martin tapped on her tent door.

"Sunny?"

She unzipped her door and he slipped inside her tent.

She shook her head helplessly. "I have leaves *everywhere*."

Martin only laughed. "The leaves do work though, don't they?"

Their group had been overwhelmed by the swarms of flies at the national park, as the insects followed the wildebeest migration. Mingati cut leaves from a local plant and they filled the truck with the branches to keep the insects away, but Sunny might have gotten carried away with how many she stuffed in her long-sleeved shirt.

"They work." She wriggled out of her long sleeves and tossed the shirt on the chair by her bed, leaving her in nothing but a thin tank top. "But they're kind of scratchy too.

Martin's eyes fell to her breasts. He stepped closer. "Maybe I should help you."

They'd fooled around some, but Sunny had been hesitant to take it any further when she knew she was leaving the next day.

What are you doing, Sunny? She could almost hear her sister's voice. *You're wasting time on a perfectly good holiday romance!*

"You'd help me?" Sunny rested her hands on his shoulders. "That's so generous."

He brushed a kiss over her mouth. "We aim to keep our guests very happy here at Karanja Safari camp." He slid his fingers along her waistband and teased the bare skin along her belly. "I would hate to think that you had any twigs or leaves left to scratch your skin."

Sunny lifted her arms. "Maybe it would be better if you took my shirt off."

Martin let out a soft sigh and pulled the tank over her head, revealing her rose-colored bra. Sunny had been waiting to wear her "sexy panties" but these weren't too ugly. She might even call them cute if they didn't have greenery and sticks stuck to them.

"Sunny." He kissed her shoulder and slid his hands to her back to unhook her bra. "You're going to kill me."

"That was not the plan," she whispered. "But can you zip up the tent flap before we go any further?"

He spun around, zipped the tent, and was back with his hands on her breasts before she could utter another word. "Your skin is impossibly soft." He took her mouth with his, kissing her to make her head spin.

She was already unbuttoning his shirt. "My skin? Yours is soft and your muscles are ridiculous."

"They're not ridiculous, they're practical."

"And don't you see how sexy that is?" She shoved her hands over his shoulders and into his shirt, tugging the material from his back.

Martin shook his arms to get rid of the shirt, all the while walking Sunny backward to the bed. "We should have gone to my tent. My bed is huge."

"This one is big enough."

He shoved his knee between her thighs and put his hands on her bottom lifting her to ride his leg. "Tonight. Spend the night with me. After dinner—"

"Yes."

That didn't mean they couldn't start in her tent. Sunny was lost in the heat of Martin's skin against her breasts. He laid her back on the bed and tasted one breast, then the next.

"I can't decide which one I like better."

She put her hand on the back of his head and arched her back. "You don't have to choose. They're a package deal."

He smiled against her skin. "Good."

"Martin?"

She put her hand on his shoulder.

"Yes?" He lifted his head and looked for her eyes. "What is it?"

You take my breath away.

She said, "It's been kind of a long time for me."

He smiled. "It's been a while for me too."

"Okay."

"Sunny, Sunny." He whispered her name over and over again. "Sweet Sunny."

She closed her eyes and made her brain stop whirling. *Live in the now, Sunny.* Her skin was on fire, every inch of it sensitized to Martin's touch. She shivered under him as he unbuttoned her pants and his, then they were laying in bed together, nothing between them and his hands exploring every inch of her.

Every. Inch.

"I didn't bring anything with me," he whispered. "So we can't—"

"We can do other things." She lifted her head. "I can... You can—there are other things we can do."

He lifted his head and smiled. "I was planning on it."

Sunny laid back and watched his head move farther down her body as his mouth explored her soft skin and his fingers explored between her thighs.

After a few minutes, she couldn't think of anything at all.

•◘•◘•◘•◘•

MARTIN WOKE up with Sunny in his arms and dread in his heart.

She was leaving.

It had only been a week of knowing her, three days of being her lover, but he was already dreading waking up tomorrow without his Sunny.

Making love to her the night before had been a

revelation, and he was kicking himself that he'd waited so long to ask her to spend the night.

But no. This was Sunny. And this was him. They weren't the quick explosion types. She was a woman who needed time.

And time was now his enemy.

She was sleeping against his shoulder, her arm draped across his chest and her dark brown hair splayed like silk on his pillow. In sleep, her lower lip stuck out in a slight pout, making her look petulant and grouchy. He smiled and moved a strand of hair from beside her nose.

She blinked her eyes open and froze. Martin waited for her to realize where she was and knew it only took a second because her body relaxed against his and she nuzzled her face into his chest.

"Last night was beautiful," she whispered. "Maybe I should stay a few more days."

Yes. Stay forever.

"I would love that, but I know you and Alice have plans to visit the beach. She might murder me in my sleep if I interrupt her holiday."

Sunny looked up and bit her lower lip, resting her chin on his chest. "You could come with us."

He smiled. "My Sunny, I cannot. I have more

guests coming tomorrow and with Alice leaving today with you, I can't be gone."

"I can come back."

His heart thumped. "You can always come back."

She blinked and he saw glassy tears in the corner of her eyes.

"No, no, no." He kissed her forehead. "No crying."

"Is this..." She blinked hard. "Is this *it*? I mean, I know people have holiday romances and things like that but I didn't think—"

"This is not that for me." He gripped her hair in his hand and held her steady. "Sunny, no. This is not the end unless... you want it to be." The thought dug into his brain. Maybe it was only a holiday romance for her. Maybe he was nothing more than a part of her vacation.

"Martin, you're not the holiday romance type of person." She blinked glassy eyes at him. "You're the real romance type of person."

He smiled and felt the fist around his heart relax. "So this isn't the end."

"But I live in America."

"And I live in Kenya." He tucked her hair behind her ear. "And we both have access to the internet. We can talk every day."

She nodded. "Okay. You're right."

"And we can visit each other."

"Yes! I would love for you to come visit me in the US. You've never been, right?"

"Never." He'd never had the urge to visit and he still didn't, but if that's what it took to see Sunny again, he'd pull out his passport and apply for a visa.

She let out a long breath. "So this isn't goodbye."

"No." He ignored the lump in his throat. "Of course not."

This isn't goodbye.

MARTIN REPEATED it to himself over and over again as he watched Sunny and Alice take off from the dirt airstrip that served the North Mara. Mingati was standing beside him.

"I thought you were smart."

Martin turned to his spotter. "What was I supposed to do? Tie her up and keep her in my tent?"

The old man shrugged. "She was happy here."

"That's illegal, Mingati." He turned and watched the plane disappearing into the distance. "This is not goodbye."

SUNNY WATCHED the airstrip disappear behind her, Martin standing near the dusty Land Cruiser. She watched until everything she'd fallen in love with had disappeared, then she looked to Alice and tried to force a smile.

"Do you want to go back?" Alice's eyebrows were up. "We don't have to go to the beach."

"Don't be silly, this is your vacation too."

"You look like a pathetic puppy."

"I'm not a pathetic puppy." She forced a smile. "I am an excited friend who is ready to party with her friend on her vacation."

Alice smirked. "You're a pathetic puppy."

"I'm not." She felt her phone buzz and she pulled it out. "Martin texted me."

"Does he miss you already?" Alice batted her eyes.

She looked at her screen and saw a line of flower emojis along with three words.

I miss you.

"This isn't goodbye." Sunny blinked back tears. "When we get to the beach, we're forming a plan, Alice."

"Oh?" Her friend raised both eyebrows. "What kind of plan? About you moving to Nairobi? I love that plan. I have been trying to get more of my friends to relocate for five years."

"No, not relocating to Nairobi. We're going to make a plan for how to have a successful long-distance romance." She quickly texted Martin back that she also missed him and she'd send him pictures of the ocean. "We're still getting to know each other. We just have to figure out how to do that with an ocean between us."

Alice snorted. "Okay. I have a Swahili program that I can recommend for you."

"Perfect!"

This could work. Why not? People met and fell in love at long distance all the time. Didn't they? She wasn't giving up on the kindest and most handsome man she'd ever met just because he lived on another continent.

They could make this work.

Chapter Seven

Nairobi, Kenya

MARTIN WOKE up and immediately reached for his phone.

Good morning, handsome.

He smiled at Sunny's message, then he checked the time in DC, hit the call button, and waited for her voice.

"Good morning," she sang.

"Good evening." He sat up in bed and swung his feet over the edge, digging his toes into the luxurious carpet of his apartment in Nairobi. "How was your day?"

"It was a day. I had a meeting with my supervisor about coming back into the office full time, but I managed to convince him that two days a week was more than adequate since almost all of my meetings are remote anyway."

"Why is that?" Birds were singing on his balcony. He pulled back the curtain and opened the French doors, breathing in the cool morning air.

"Why did he want me to come into the office more?"

"That is no question. Any sane person would want to have you around more. Why are your meetings remote?"

She was silent for a moment, and Martin noticed it again. Sunny was unaccustomed to receiving compliments. What on earth was wrong with American men? Was her family unappreciative of her quiet goodness? He was baffled how this woman could be so overlooked.

Sunny continued. "Most of the bank's fund managers are in New York, so while the actuarial department where I work is in DC, most of the people who want the information I research are in New York."

Martin rose and walked to the bathroom, putting his phone on speaker. "Did they ever consider moving you to New York?"

"They've suggested it, but like I said, most of my

work can be done remotely. I don't want to have to pay for a New York apartment if I don't have to. And all my family is in DC." She stopped to take a breath. "How are the elephants?"

He smiled. "Probably as destructive as ever, but I'm in Nairobi right now. I flew in yesterday afternoon for that meeting with my father."

"Oh, that's right! I forgot. How's Nairobi? I heard the birds, so I assumed that you were at the camp."

"I have a nice balcony here in the city, and the caretaker waters the garden, so the birds are very happy out there. The compound where my apartment is has a beautiful garden behind it. I'll send you pictures."

His apartment in the Karen neighborhood in Nairobi was actually the second story west wing of a large mansion owned by a British family who were friends of Errol's. Martin had been eager to leave his parents' home, even though there was plenty of room, and this family was looking for an influx of cash to keep their old house running. It was a perfect match, especially since Martin wasn't in the city full time.

"Send me all the pictures," Sunny pleaded with him. "Everything is hot and humid here. If I even step out of my apartment, I'm dripping."

"So summers in Washington DC are warm?" He carefully trimmed around the short beard that he had decided to grow out. "On the positive side, that must mean winters are mild and pleasant."

"No. Winters are kind of cold and slushy. It usually snows, but then it melts and gets all dirty. Then it freezes."

He frowned. "So when is a good time to visit?"

"Roughly two weeks in the spring and two weeks in the fall."

His eyebrows went up. "Why did your country choose a place with unpleasant weather as its capitol?"

"I really don't know."

He considered when he could possibly visit her. The fall was coming and the camp would slow down. Perhaps the fall window of pleasant weather was a good idea. It was still months away; he wished he could see her tomorrow. Next week. Next month at the latest.

"I miss you." He took a deep breath. "Thank you for texting every morning. It's lovely to wake up and see a message from you."

"Thank you too." He could hear the smile in her voice. "I love getting your messages when I wake up too."

"I have to leave for my meeting if I don't want to be late. Have a wonderful night and sleep well."

"Video chat in my morning?"

Martin smiled. "That sounds perfect."

"Okay. Um... *tutaonana*."

"Whaaat?" Martin laughed. "Listen to you!"

"Did I get it right? I was trying to say 'see you later.'"

"You got it; you sound great. Are you learning Swahili?"

"Alice sent me a program to learn, so I'm trying."

"I love it." He felt his heart melt even more. She was wonderful and he wanted her every day. All day. "Tutaonana, Sunny. I wish I didn't have to go."

"Go, go. Don't be late for your meeting. I'll talk to you in my morning."

He hung up the phone and immediately sent her a flower emoji. She sent him one back, then he rushed out the door and headed to meet his father.

•◘•◘•◘•◘•

"YOUR EARNINGS ARE CONSISTENT." His father paged through the print-outs in a manila folder. "The challenge will be to increase visitors during your shoulder seasons to bump up the average to make it through the off-season."

Martin flipped through the PDF of the profit and loss statement on his tablet. "We're uniquely advantaged with that because we're partnered with the local landowners. Grazing the cattle through the conservancy keeps the tall grass down, which makes the grazing animals content to stay longer. The populations aren't huge, but the big draws are consistent and Errol and I think that discounted rates during that time will attract more bargain-minded visitors or repeat guests who would be more interested in the resident populations of wildlife. The elephants stay. The lions stay. The cheetahs are always there."

His father grunted, which was all that Martin had come to expect as far as feedback went.

John Karanja had been skeptical of the loan Martin had requested for the business, so Martin had been forced to put his father's name on the business in order to get the loan. It was still better than going to banks, though Martin was trying desperately to get outside funding so he could buy his father's portion of the business and finally have something that was all his own.

"The Karanja name stands for quality, professionalism, and a level of elite service." His father was still staring at the P&L. "I have been impressed by the quality of your furnishings, your social media presence, and the experience you are providing. The food has excellent reviews and the service has gained a consistent reputation for quality."

He nodded. "Thank you, Father."

"And yet, I hear a rumor that you formed a relationship with a guest while she was visiting the camp." He looked up and Martin saw the disapproval in his father's gaze. "You are not Errol Canberry, Martin. You cannot take liberties like this and your mother would be embarrassed if she knew. We didn't raise you to carry on with guests. That's not the kind of family you come from."

Martin lifted his chin. "I met Susannah Randolph as my camp manager's school friend. The fact that she was a guest at the camp was—"

"Incontrovertible." His father snapped the folder shut. "Undeniable. Martin—"

"No." He raised a hand. "I am not going to put my relationship with Sunny in the same category as Errol's affair-of-the-month, and I won't have you thinking that it's anything like what you're imagining. Sunny is a very special woman, and we are taking time to get to know one another."

His father raised both eyebrows. "Are you saying that you're still in contact with this woman?"

"As I said, we are getting to know each other."

Martin smiled. "She's a lovely and accomplished woman."

"So she is in Nairobi?"

Martin looked down at his tablet and scanned the third quarter projections. "No, she lives in Washington DC."

John Karanja laughed a little. "Son, I don't want to disappoint you but the likelihood of anything—"

"Father, I am a grown man." He looked up. "I don't need romantic advice."

"She's not Kenyan."

Martin set his tablet to the side. "I am aware of that."

"She's not even African."

"No, she is not."

"And does she know who your family is?"

Does she know you're wealthy? It was the unspoken question every time he met a woman. "She knows we own the safari camp, yes."

"And a chain of luxury hotels. And property along the coast. And we're building the new resort in the Seychelles. And—"

"I don't think she's interested in that; I believe she has a very good job of her own."

His father folded his hands. "And what does she

do, Martin? Is she a... a barista? A schoolteacher? An internet influencer perhaps? Is she—?"

"She's an actuarial advisor for Smith, Hagner, and Warner, the investment bank. I'm sure you've heard of them. She analyzes risk potential for investment prospects. I believe her family lives in Chevy Chase, Maryland. Have you heard of it?"

Martin couldn't lie. It was gratifying to see his father's eyes narrow when he realized that Sunny didn't fit the mold he was imagining.

"So she analyzes risk." John Karanja took a deep breath. "As I am sure she is doing right now with a relationship started on a holiday with a man who lives on the other side of the world."

And there was the dig again. "Whatever the risk is, I am willing to take it. And it's none of your business. If and when Sunny returns to Nairobi to visit, I expect you to treat her with respect."

His father knew when he'd gone too far. "I'm not saying she's not a lovely woman, Martin, but I don't want you to get your hopes up. What do you think is going to happen? You think this American professional is going to give up her life in Washington and move to Kenya?" He smiled indulgently. "Your life and your work are here, son. You are the future of Karanja Enterprises."

"And I have never shirked that responsibility." Hundreds, perhaps thousands of employees soon, depended on continuity, wise leadership, and a steady hand from the head of Karanja. Martin knew that his father's retirement was years and years away, but he also knew that he was the only one in line to succeed him.

"Then think, Martin. Think about your future and hers." His father tapped a finger on the manila folder. "A relationship can be good and still not be the right thing. That is life."

•◘•◘•◘•◘•

Washington D.C., USA

LULU BLINKED HER EYES. "Wait, the man you met in Kenya?"

"He's the owner of the safari camp where Alice works." Sunny was having drinks with her sister after her last day in the office that week. She really needed to get Kevin to let her work remotely all the time. Life in the office was draining and she only got half the work done that she did at home. She rubbed both her thumbs on her temples. "And yes, he's Kenyan."

Her sister blinked. "But you've been home for like two months."

Sunny frowned. "And?"

"You're still texting your holiday hookup?"

"He's not a holiday hook up." Sunny almost laughed, but her headache was too piercing. "I wonder if I should just go home. This headache is not getting any better."

"You need to drink more water." She pushed her full glass of water with no ice and lemon across the table at the wine bar in Falls Church City. "Have you eaten anything today?"

Sunny blinked. "I had breakfast."

"It's seven o'clock, Sunny!" Lulu waved down a server and asked for a menu. "What is with you? It's not like you to forget to eat."

"I don't know." She did know. She was at the office and she was afraid to open her door lest a flood of coworkers come into her office and distract her from the project she was working on, so she'd worked through lunch. "I forgot to bring a lunch and I was in the office today."

"You and the remote working thing." Lulu shook her head. "It's not healthy. You're already an introvert and working from home just makes it worse."

"I heartily disagree."

"Can we get back to the Kenyan guy you've been texting for two months?"

"Almost three now."

"It was a fun holiday romance, Sunny. It doesn't have to mean anything more than that. I swear, you take everything too seriously."

"I'm not taking it too seriously." Which was a complete lie. She was half in love with Martin. Maybe more.

Definitely more.

"I mean, from what you told me, the man is handsome, rich, and fit. He might have girlfriends on every continent for all you know. He meets people from all over the world all the time."

Her sister must have saw when the suspicion pierced Sunny's heart.

"Oh sweetie, no." Lulu reached across the table and took her hand. "You're gorgeous and smart and have so much going for you. He could not find better anywhere in the world!"

Sunny sipped her water. "But...?"

"If you lived in the same place then it would probably be an amazing relationship."

"People have long distance relationships, Lu. It's not... You and Chaz were long distance for two years when he was in grad school."

"But we didn't start out that way. We had a relationship first, happened to have to go long distance for a while—three hours apart, by the way, not twenty-five or something."

"Fifteen hours by air." *Not counting layovers.*

"I'm just saying, no one *starts* a relationship with someone on another continent."

Sunny was silent, remembering the message from Martin that morning. It was the only thing that had brightened her day when she knew she'd had to go into the office. "What if…?" She swallowed the lump of doubt in her throat. "What if we do?"

Lulu felt sorry for her, and Sunny couldn't stand it when her big sister looked at her with pity.

"Just because you didn't do it doesn't mean we can't." She remembered Martin's laugh and brilliant smile when she saw him over the video chat the other night. He'd grown his beard out and it suited him. He looked even more like an adventurous explorer. He'd been teasing her about shaving it off when he came to visit so he didn't scratch her face and she'd protested that he needed to keep it.

"Isn't it possible?" Sunny blinked back the tears and sipped Lulu's water. "I mean, why not? He's going to come for a visit when the camp slows down. He's not hitting the clubs in Nairobi every weekend, Lu.

Alice says he works all the time and she said she's never seen him date a guest before."

"Okay, good." Lulu shrugged. "*Good*. I'd love to meet him when he visits." She was still skeptical, Sunny could tell. "When is he thinking about flying over?"

"Probably the beginning of November. That's when things usually slow down."

"Good. Cool. He sounds very sweet. You know me, I'm just protective. I don't want this guy scamming you."

"He's not like that."

"Okay."

Sunny knew that Lulu thought she was naive and inexperienced. And... in a way she was. She hadn't been like her sister in college with boyfriends and a huge social life. Sunny had only had a few friends; she believed in quality over quantity. And since many of her friends from school lived overseas, she didn't hang out with them regularly.

But then there was Martin.

He was sweet. And kind. And thoughtful. He'd called a florist in Arlington the week before and sent her Tahiti daffodils because she'd mentioned reading about them in a book.

He was concerned two nights ago when she had a bandaid over a paper cut on her hand and wouldn't let it alone until she promised him that it really was a surface wound.

He mailed her a stuffed elephant two weeks before that, taping a plastic straw to the elephant's trunk with a note: Laxodonta africana, *the African bush elephant, here in its native habitat, which would be digging up my water pipes for the third time this year.*

It had been so cute, Sunny had called him immediately, forgetting that it was still the middle of the night for him. Martin hadn't minded. They'd talked for an hour before he had to hang up.

"He's not like that, Lu." Sunny reached across the table and squeezed her sister's hand. "I promise. When you meet him, you'll understand. Martin isn't like other guys. He's special."

Chapter Eight

MARTIN SAT in the office-grey chair with stained upholstery that tilted precariously to the right and stared at the visa official across the desk.

"Are you serious?"

"I'm sorry, but you're going to need a letter from your employer saying that you will still have a job when you return from the United States and frankly, you don't own enough property here in Kenya to qualify for a tourist visa."

The words slipped out of Martin's mouth before he could stop them. "I'm sorry, but do you know who I am?"

The man in the poorly fitted suit sat back in his chair and lifted his chin. "I'm the man who gets to decide if you have a tourist visa to the United States,

Mr...." He looked at the application. "Mr. Karamja."

"*Karanja*. Martin Karanja, owner of Karanja Safari Company and Vice President of Karanja Enterprises."

"Which is owned by who?" The man spread his hands. "I don't see any documents here that indicate you own *anything*, sir. A car. That's it. You have a lease, but you don't own a house. Your Safari company is only five years old and it's owned jointly by you, a Mr. Errol Carberry, and your father. You don't own the land that you operate on, you have outstanding loans at two banks, and very little in savings."

"I can't believe this." His father's obstinacy about putting things in Martin's name was biting him *again*. "Sir, I don't mean to be disrespectful but if you would call the banks where I owe the money or simply call the ambassador, for that matter—"

"Visas to the United States are not handed out because of who one knows, Mr. Karamja." The man was flushed and angry now. "It's my responsibility to take into account the safety and the security of the United States of America."

Martin was getting angry too. "What do you think I'm going to do when I go to the US? You think I'm going to leave my very comfortable life and all my businesses here to get a job paying minimum wage as an illegal migrant in a crowded city with weather no one would envy?"

The visa official raised his chin even higher. "People overstay visas every day, Mr. Karamja."

Martin snorted. "This is absurd." He rose. "I have traveled to India, Japan, Singapore, Fiji, Dubai, and a dozen other places in my life—"

"On business visas related to your father's company, *not* as a tourist."

"And all I'm trying to do today is secure a visa to visit a friend in Arlington, Virginia." Martin sneered. "And you think I'm going to be *tempted* by the irresistible draw of America to abandon my life here? You are ridiculous."

The man stamped something across Martin's application and set it to the side. "Visa application denied. The United States of America does not believe you have enough permanent ties to your home country to be assured of your return to Kenya and considers you an overstay risk."

Martin narrowed his eyes. "And my application fee?"

It cost a pretty penny to apply for a US tourist visa. It was nothing for someone with Martin's resources, but the majority of Kenyans in the line outside didn't have the resources he did. For most of them, the dollars it cost to apply for a visa would be a significant sacrifice.

“Application fees are for processing your application and are non-refundable.”

“How convenient for you.” Martin turned and walked out of the office. He walked out of the building, passing the line of visa applicants arriving for their interviews. Dozens and dozens of them were waiting silently, some for business reasons, some for immigration purposes, but probably countless others were wanting, like him, to visit friends or family overseas.

And they said that bankers were thieves.

He took his phone out and called Errol.

“Karanja!” His friend’s voice was jolly. “So have you bought your ticket yet?”

“My visa application was denied.”

Errol laughed, then he fell silent when Martin didn’t join in. “What?”

“Denied, Carberry. They didn’t think I had enough permanent ties to Kenya to return.” Martin wanted to laugh. He wanted to cry. Sometimes his permanent ties to Kenya felt more like ropes binding him. He walked to United Nations Avenue and waited in the shade of a tree for his driver to circle the block and come pick him up.

"That's ridiculous. What about all the other times you've traveled?"

"Apparently because I'm only going as a tourist—"

"So figure out some business reason to go to the States and see Sunny instead. Who cares? Martin, you're mad for this woman. I've never seen you—"

"You think I want to go to a country that would treat me this way?" He glanced back at the growing line of people. "That would treat any Kenyan this way? It's insulting. I don't need to visit a place that doesn't want me."

"Sunny wants you." Errol's voice was suddenly serious. "And you want her. You've been happier the last three months than any other time I've known you. You're in love with her. It's worth it to—"

"I've been living in some fantasy." He saw his driver crest the hill. "I've got to go. I'll be back in the Mara tomorrow afternoon. Have one of the guides come pick me up on the 2:30 flight."

He texted Sunny when he got in the car. *Call me when you wake up.*

She texted back immediately. *I'm awake. How did the interview go? When are you coming?*

Martin hesitated for a moment, then he hit the call button.

"Hey, how did it go?"

She sounded sleepy and sweet and Martin almost wanted to reassure her that he would fix it somehow, but there was nothing to fix. He wasn't going to be visiting her in Virginia.

"They denied my tourist visa," he said. "They think I'm at risk to overstay."

She laughed, then like Errol, she realized he was serious. "Wait, what?"

"They think I'm going to overstay my visa, get a job driving a cab, and live in a house with a dozen other African migrants."

"Did they say that?" She sounded horrified.

"Of course not, they didn't need to. It was obvious from the official's face what he was thinking." Martin felt humiliated just telling her.

"Wait, they can't—Is there some way you can appeal this? That's ridiculous."

"I agree." He snapped at his driver to take him back to his apartment.

"What do you want to do? We can't let one bureaucrat stop you from coming to—"

"Sunny, can you imagine yourself living in Kenya?" He blurted out the question that had been plaguing his mind for weeks. "Not just for a holiday, not for a summer or a season, but all of the time?"

The silence on the other side of the line was vast.

For the first time, Martin felt the worlds between them. His life. Her life. His family obligations. Her family obligations. Two different lives. Two different futures.

"Because I can't live in the United States," he continued. "I don't have a home there or a future there, and I'm never going to have one. My life is here. My home is here. My responsibilities are here. And I have many responsibilities. Do you understand that?"

She finally spoke, but her voice was small. "Yes. I understand that."

"So what are we doing?" He felt his heart breaking as the silence on the other line dragged on. "We are not children."

"What are you saying?" Her voice was barely over a whisper.

What *was* he saying? His anger and his humiliation had collided with his pride. Every doubt his father had raised didn't seem unreasonable now. His father was right. They lived in different worlds. Martin wanted a partner, a wife, a family. Not right away, but he was thirty-three. He didn't have forever.

"I'm saying that while I have very strong feelings for you, I don't have the time to devote myself to a relationship that has no future," he said. "And neither do you. That's not what I want. And you deserve a partner who can be there for you. Not just on the phone but in your life."

"Are you breaking up with me?" She sounded lost and hurt. Martin was kicking himself, but he knew he was doing the right thing.

A relationship can be good and still not be the right thing.

Martin closed his eyes. "I'm saying that what we had was beautiful, and I would not trade it for anything." He swallowed the lump in his throat. "But I think it's time to move on."

•◘•◘•◘•◘•

SUNNY STARED at the short message on the screen.

Happy birthday. I hope you are having a wonderful day. You deserve every good thing.

Seeing a message from Martin should have made her want to throw her phone against the wall, but it just made her impossibly sad.

I miss you.

I miss your smile.

I miss your laugh.

I miss hearing about your day.

I miss hearing the birds on your balcony.

She was twenty-nine and instead of the big party she'd been planning in her head when Martin came to visit her, she was spending the day at the office, then meeting her sister at her favorite wine bar before they joined their parents, Lulu's husband Chaz, and her two-year-old niece at her parents' club for a very civilized dinner.

In the three weeks since Martin had broken things off, Sunny had buried herself in work, only telling Lulu about it the week before.

She had to admire her sister's restraint. She hadn't said 'I told you so' even once.

"Do you want me to fly to Kenya and beat him up?"

Sunny had tried on the mental picture of her five foot, two-inch sister—who probably weighed one hundred twenty pounds sopping wet—standing up to Martin's broad shoulders and near six-foot height.

It made her feel slightly better that Lulu had taken her side, but not really. The problem was... Martin was right and she missed him.

His life was there, and his visa rejection was only the final sign that what everyone had been saying was correct: you couldn't have a long-distance relationship if it had no future.

Her phone started buzzing with a video call.

Please don't let it be him...

She closed her eyes, willing it not to be her ex... whatever he was. It felt strange to call Martin her ex-boyfriend when they'd never really had a chance to be together in the first place.

Luckily, it was Alice.

"Happy birthday, my friend!" Alice's giant smile filled the screen and it was impossible for Sunny not to smile. "Ah! How are we twenty-nine *already*?"

"We didn't die, so getting older was the only option?"

"Oh, someone is in a mood." Alice stuck out her lips in a pout. "What on earth is going on? No one tells me anything! It's forever since I've talked to you. I go home for a couple weeks to help my sister with her new baby, then I come back to a cranky boss and a moping friend. What happened?"

"I didn't know your sister had a baby. Congratulations. Boy or girl?"

"Don't change the subject! I've got like thirty-seven nieces and nephews, will you tell me what's going on with you and Martin?"

"Nothing." She shrugged. "I think we both care about each other a lot, but we realized that it just wasn't realistic to build a relationship with no future." She cleared her throat. "His life and responsibilities are in Kenya and I respect that. And like you said, we're getting older; we need to be intentional about relationships."

Alice stared at the screen. "What kind of bullshit is this? You two are in love with each other."

Sunny felt the tears starting to well in her eyes. "Alice, it's my birthday. Please don't make me—"

"Are you in love with Martin?"

"No! That's ridiculous. You don't fall in love with someone after a week."

"It hasn't been a week, it's been over four months. You two were talking every day. You were taking language lessons. He was going to come visit—"

"His visa got rejected; he can't come visit."

And yes, she was in love with him. She'd fallen in love with Martin one phone call at a time, over meals shared via video chat and silly presents sent in the mail. She loved his kindness and his humor. She loved his thoughtfulness and his passion for his work and his employees.

She loved him, but it didn't matter.

"Oh for goodness sake!" Alice burst out. "Most visa applications get rejected the first time. My own mother had to apply three times before she could come visit me when I was in school. But he applies once, gets his pride hurt and—"

"No, it wasn't just that. Afterward, he called me

and he asked me if I could see living in Kenya long term and I... I didn't know. I couldn't give him an answer, Alice. That's when he said the thing about our relationship having no future and—"

"Wait, when did he call you?"

"Right after they rejected his application."

"And he put you on the spot like that? Asked if you'd move to Kenya just like that?"

"It's a reasonable question." She stood and walked to the bathroom. She was going to have to go into the office that day and she had to be presentable. "I can't argue with him. That's a completely fair question."

"But he didn't give you any time to think about it, he just threw that at you and when you didn't respond the way he wanted, he gave up and now he's moping around the camp like a sad little boy and snapping at Errol and me if we set one foot out of place."

Sunny closed her eyes. "I'm sorry. I should have never gotten involved with your boss."

"This isn't your fault!" She muttered something under her breath. "Ooh, I want to punch men sometimes; they are so stupid."

"Martin isn't stupid."

"Of course he is. Normally? No. But about this, he is. He asks you a question like that—a very big question!—with no warning and then jumps to conclusions when you don't immediately answer as he wants. I mean, have you thought about moving to Kenya since he asked you? People move all the time; I don't know why he assumed you wouldn't."

Of course she'd thought about it more. Once Martin had put the idea in her head, it had been hard to think of anything else.

She had friends scattered all over the world. Alice was in Kenya. Leslie was working in Spain. Her roommate from freshman year had married a man from Singapore and they were living in Indonesia, working in software design, and expecting a baby.

Of course she *could* move.

Alice was in Kenya. They could share an apartment again when Alice was in the city. Sunny had no idea what kind of visa she would need to live and work in the country, but surely there were options.

"I could live in Kenya," Sunny said softly.

"But he didn't even give you time to think about it. See? Men are stupid."

She could find a new job that allowed her to be completely remote.

She had a trust fund and a healthy savings account.

Her family was wonderful, but they all had their own lives.

None of her friends lived in the area anymore.

"I could live in Kenya." Sunny set down her hairbrush and stared at her reflection in the mirror. "I could live in *Kenya*."

Beautiful, warm Kenya where it didn't snow and the air was clear and birds were everywhere. Where a visit to the national park meant seeing elephants and zebras instead of pigeons and skunks.

"Alice, I *could* live in Kenya."

"Of course you could! But I don't blame you for not wanting to be bothered with that man. Oh, this makes me so mad. He is in love with you but his head is made of rocks, I tell you. *Rocks*."

Sunny turned and looked at her apartment. Two rooms, a tiny kitchen, no balcony. She owned it, but she could sublet it and pay for an apartment in Nairobi that had outdoor space.

She could grow flowers and listen to birds from her own balcony. She could fly to the Mara to see Alice on the weekend. She was already learning Swahili. If she was living in Kenya, then she could visit Tanzania too. She could eat Ethiopian food in *Ethiopia*. She could fly to India. She could swim in the Indian Ocean and vacation in Thailand.

She *could* move to Kenya. If not for Martin, then maybe just for herself. She could be a woman who did that. What was the worst that could happen?

What was the worst that could happen? Sunny thought long and hard.

It wouldn't work and she hated it.

And then?

She could move back.

"Alice, I need to get off the phone." She closed her eyes. "Please don't mention to Martin that we talked, okay? I need to think about this and maybe.... I don't know."

Alice stopped muttering under her breath. "Wait, are you seriously going to move to Nairobi?"

"I don't know." She took a deep breath. "I can't say yes for sure but... I'm not saying no."

Chapter Nine

MARTIN DIDN'T DRINK ALONE. He wasn't much of a drinker at all, but he enjoyed a cocktail with friends, a whiskey with a guest, or a glass of champagne to celebrate an occasion.

He was sitting along in his tent and a third into a bottle of Johnny Walker when Errol came to find him.

"Karanja?"

Martin closed his eyes and said nothing.

"I know you're in there and I know you're alone; I'm coming in."

He didn't care anymore. It was Sunny's birthday and he should have been celebrating with her. She was twenty-nine this year and she'd talked about feeling nervous about the change from her twenties to her thirties.

They'd had long conversations about the shifting feelings of growing up and growing older. Transitioning from young person to full fledged adult. The way that parents changed and expectations shifted about life and success.

He and Sunny had talked about everything. Their jobs, their families, their hopes for the future. He'd had a relationship this gem of a human being who wanted to know everything about him and he wanted the same. He wanted to know what had made her laugh that day and what made her unhappy.

He was an idiot.

Errol unzipped the tent flap and caught sight of him. "Good lord, Karanja, this isn't like you. You look like me."

"I don't want to talk about it." He set his near-empty glass on the desk.

"Have you called her to apologize? Have you said that you were angry at the embassy and took it out on her? Have you told her that you received an apology from the ambassador less than a week later?"

"That was my father's doing, not mine." John Karanja had been furious that the US government had questioned Martin's intentions. It had actually led to a helpful discussion about transferring the safari company and some of the other assets that Martin managed into his name instead of the company's, but the damage had been done.

He'd broken her trust.

"She doesn't want to live here," Martin said. "Especially not now. As much as I miss her—as much as I regret my words to her—the fact remains that there's an ocean and a continent between us, Carberry. I can't change that."

"So figure out a way to make it work! Living in the United States could be...fun?" Saying the words made Errol look like he was in pain.

Martin cocked his head and stared at him. "Really?"

His partner pulled up a chair and sat across from him. "Even if it was just for a while, you could try it. Maybe you and your father could start a hotel there. Give you and Sunny time together so you can convince her to move here." Errol clapped his hands. "That's the best idea I've had yet. Leave this place for me and Alice to run—you know we're capable—start a business in America for a while, then use that time to convince Sunny to move here. Problem solved."

"Carberry—"

"You're a miserable shit without her, and I'm saying that with love."

"Clearly."

"You're a pain in the arse to me and Alice when you're like this. She's going to quit if you don't change your mind and you know we're sunk without her. She's the one who makes this place run."

Martin had no answer to that, because it was true.

"You think any job or business or legacy is worth it if you're miserable? Listen to me, because you know I know what I'm talking about."

Martin was about to pick up the whiskey again, but he set it down. "I'm listening."

"If you aren't with someone you love, what's the point?" Errol shook his head. "I have been looking my whole life for someone who looks at me the way that Sunny Randolph looks at you. Do you know how lucky you are?"

"Yes." He put his hands over his face and wished he'd left two glasses of whiskey in the bottle. "I know I was lucky, and then I fucked it up."

"So fix it!"

"I sent her a text message this morning for her birthday and she didn't respond." He'd been kicking himself since their last conversation. "She hasn't responded to any of my messages."

"Did any of those messages start with 'Sunny, I am an idiot and I love you?'"

No. He looked up at Errol. "Do I really need to say that?"

Errol crossed his arms and stared at Martin. "Do you want her back?"

Yes.

Desperately.

He needed to hear her voice, even if she was angry with him.

"I want her back."

"Then fly to America and make it happen." Errol grabbed the bottle of Johnny Walker. "And share your whiskey; don't be rude."

•◘•◘•◘•◘•

THE WOMAN at immigration looked at her passport. "And you are here for a working holiday?"

Sunny forced a smile. "Yes, thank you." She was exhausted from lack of sleep; she hadn't been able to settle down for a minute on the flight.

She was nervous. She was excited!

Her mother was nearly hysterical.

Her sister was the only one who seemed to understand exactly why Sunny had rented out her apartment and decided to move to the other side of the world a week after her birthday.

Do it now. You'll never regret it. You'll only regret if you don't try.

The immigration officer continued, "And you understand that this visa is valid for ninety days only, and it can be extended via the office of immigration?"

"I understand."

"Your lodgings?" The woman looked at her paperwork. "I see you have a house rental for only two weeks?"

"I have a friend from here, and she's going to help me look for something more long-term." Sunny's head was starting to swim.

"I see." The woman smiled. "And your employer is in the United States?"

"Yes, I won't be working for any Kenyan companies while I'm here. I'm simply working online for my US employer."

"Thank you." Finally, the woman stamped her passport and handed it back with a smile. "Welcome to Kenya, Miss Randolph."

"Thank you. *Jambo*."

The immigration officer smiled. "Ah! You're learning Swahili? That's excellent."

"I'm trying." This time Sunny's smile was genuine and she felt a well of gratitude at the friendliness of this utter stranger. "I really love Kenya."

The officer's eyes softened. "I'm sure you will have a wonderful time here. Especially with your friend to show you around."

"Thank you." Sunny gathered her documents and tucked them into her shoulder bag, then she grabbed the handle of her roller bag and headed in the direction of the baggage claim. She had two massive suitcases packed and she was still thinking about how she was going to get them in a cab and up the stairs to her second story flat when she heard someone call her name.

"Sunny?"

She turned and saw Martin standing across the hallway.

Her eyes went wide. "Martin."

He was frozen in place, dressed in a pair of slacks and a polo shirt. He had a backpack and a roll-on bag, clearly ready to travel.

He looks amazing.

Was she dreaming? Had Alice told him she was coming? She'd planned on contacting him when she settled in, but she hadn't prepared what she was going to say.

"I'm..." She stammered. "Uh—"

"What are you doing here?" Martin walked across

the hallway, looking as shocked as Sunny felt. "You're here. Why are you here?"

Because I'm almost thirty and I'm in love with you. But not only because of that. She opened her mouth. Closed it. Opened it again, but all that came out was... "Hi."

He stared at her. "You're in Kenya."

"I am."

Martin lifted a boarding pass. "I'm flying to America."

She frowned. "They gave you a visa?"

"It's a business visa and I received an apology from —You're in Nairobi!"

A passenger with a large backpack bumped Sunny's shoulder. "And you're flying to America?"

"No! Yes." He blinked. "I'm supposed to. My flight leaves—but you're here."

Crowds were maneuvering around them and Sunny was starting to feel like a stalled car in traffic. "I should go get my luggage." She gestured in the direction foot traffic was flowing. "Do you need to make a flight? Because I'm going to be here for three months, so if you—"

"Three months?" A laugh burst from his mouth. "You're here for three months?"

"Yeah." She started to back away down the

terminal and Martin followed at a short distance. "I was going to call you when I got settled in so if you're flying to the US for work—"

"I am not flying to America for work, I am flying there because I love you."

Sunny froze and Martin kept walking toward her.

A few people in the terminal around them laughed. One woman yelped as if someone had stood on her toe, and two businessmen turned to each other and chuckled quietly.

"Tell me I'm not too late." Martin kept walking toward her. "What should I do to apologize?"

Tears sprang into Sunny's eyes. This was nothing like she'd imagined. In fact, being the center of attention was generally a recurring nightmare.

But this time, she wasn't alone. Martin was with her.

"You asked me on the phone if I could see myself living in Kenya." She blinked back tears. "Permanently. And I wasn't really awake when I answered."

"So you flew to Nairobi?" Martin suddenly seemed to realize that they were the subject of stares and public amusement. "Come with me." He grabbed her hand and walked her toward the baggage claim, turning down a corridor that looked a little more private. "What about your work? Your family?"

"I told you I do most of it remotely anyway. I told my boss I was going to quit to try living in Kenya and he was kind of desperate when I said that, so he told me I could go one hundred percent remote, which I was kind of hoping for because I didn't want to have to find a new job if I didn't have to, but I also got a raise, which I was definitely not expecting." She looked around, and reality suddenly cut through the exhaustion. "You're here." She looked up and smiled. "I missed you."

Martin let out a strangled laugh. "I missed you every hour of every day you were gone."

"Me too."

"Sunny." He looked around, then he leaned down and captured her mouth in a fierce kiss. "Let's get out of here," he whispered against her lips. "I can't believe you're here."

"What about your flight?"

"I was only going to see you." He put an arm around her, grabbed the shoulder bag from her arm, and took her suitcase in hand. "I'll call my driver to meet us."

They walked past security and everyone seemed to move out of Martin's way. It helped that he was tall and seemed to know where he was going.

"Can you call Alice and let her know that Trevor doesn't need to pick me up?"

"Who is Trevor?" Martin looked down with a stern frown.

"Friend of Alice's." She leaned into his shoulder and felt the exhaustion starting to take over. "I did not sleep at all on this flight."

He rubbed her back. "You must be exhausted."

"And my rental is on the second floor." She yawned. "I don't know how I'm going to get my suit-cases upstairs. I don't think there's an elevator."

"I'm not taking you to your rental place." Martin secured his arm around her waist. "I'm taking you home."

Chapter Ten

SUNNY WOKE to the sound of birds singing on the balcony. A warm breeze touched her face and she heard low humming in the distance. She opened her eyes and the sun reached across crisp white sheets, inching toward her body.

She was still wearing her leggings and the oversized t-shirt she'd dressed in the day before. Or had it been two days? She sat up and rubbed her eyes, looking around the room.

Sunny was in a lavish bedroom with dark wood floors, lush Persian carpets, and white walls dotted with bright modern art. There was a distinctly masculine feel to the room with dark wooden shades covering most of the windows, a long dresser with a collection of heavy fragrance bottles and a mahogany valet stand with a suit jacket hanging from the back.

Where was she?

Memories creeped in. A dark SUV at the airport with Martin barking at a driver in a black suit. Calling Alice to tell her she had arrived. Martin on the phone with Alice, arguing in Swahili. Half a dozen voices chattering around her as Martin ushered her into his apartment.

He'd carried her. Sunny blinked. Martin had carried her into his room and taken her shoes off before the comfort of a soft, flat surface convinced her body to finally give in.

Now she was staring at a picture of her in one frame and another of the two of them from their last night in the Mara that Alice had taken with Martin's phone. She'd had the same picture in her bedroom until Martin had broken up with her.

There was a tapping at the door and it creaked open on shiny brass hinges.

Martin appeared carrying a tray and wearing a huge smile. "You're awake."

Sunny stretched up and covered a massive yawn with her hand. "Hi."

"Yes, you said that at the airport." Martin was still grinning. "You're in Nairobi."

She blinked and watched him set a tray down with what looked like a glass of juice, a cup of tea, and some fruit. "Yes."

"Alice didn't tell me."

"I told her not to."

That got rid of the smile. Martin turned and sat at the foot of the bed. "I don't blame you for that. I was... not at my best the last time we spoke."

Sunny didn't say anything.

He reached over and put a hand on her foot. "I would never assume anything about our relationship simply because you are here. I wouldn't assume your motives or your—"

"I came for you." Sunny said the words quietly. "And for me."

His hand closed around her foot. "Truly?"

"Maybe I'm naive or dumb or... I don't know. Maybe I misunderstood you the last time we spoke."

"I am so sor—"

"Let me finish."

Martin nodded, but kept this hand on her foot.

"I don't think the problem was ever the way we felt about each other. At least, I don't think so. The problem was imaging a future." She kept her eyes on his hand; the graceful long fingers rubbed the arch of her foot. "We had so little time together, and then we were talking every day, but it was only for a few months. Everything still felt new. So when you asked me if I could see myself living here full time, it felt sudden. It was hard for me to imagine it."

Martin nodded, but he stayed silent.

"And then I did think about it, and I realized that I've been making the expected choice all my life. I'm twenty-nine and I work at the same bank I interned at in college. I live in the same apartment. I let other peoples' expectations dictate what I thought my life should look like. And I don't need to." She smiled. "I can imagine something bigger now."

"Are your parents upset with you for moving? I don't want to cause a rift in your family. That is the last thing I want."

Sunny narrowed her eyes. "I don't think anyone expected me to stay in DC forever. Maybe I just thought they did." She looked into his eyes. "I came here for me, Martin, but I also came for you. I don't know if I want to live in Kenya forever, but I can try. Why not try?"

"My Sunny." He leaned forward. "Can I kiss you?"

"I would be really disappointed if you didn't."

He bent forward, gripping her foot, sliding his

hand up her ankle, and trailing his fingers up her thigh until he was leaning over her. He slowly lowered his lips to hers and it was everything Sunny remembered and more.

More because there was more between them. More understanding, more intimacy, more emotion.

I am not flying to America for work, I am flying there because I love you.

"I love you too," she whispered.

"Oh Sunny." He wrapped her in his arms, hiked her leg over his hips, and held her, nearly crushing her to his chest. "I was flying to Washington and I had no idea if you would even speak to me, but I had to try." His hands were moving over her back, cupping her bottom and gripping it as he pulled her closer. "I missed you so much."

"I probably really need a shower."

"I don't care." He kissed her over and over, running his hands over her back, her bottom. Another hand slid into her hair, tracing her temple, her ear, the line of her jaw. "I feel like you're going to disappear if I let go of you."

"I'm here." She felt her body wake up, the scent of his skin bringing her back to stolen moments and nights in the Mara. She slid her hands down his flat stomach and cupped his erection through his linen pants.

Martin surrounded her. He stretched his leg out and nudged the French doors to the patio closed. "I'll show you everything... later."

"I missed you so much." Desire was starting to feel frantic. She wanted him. She needed him. She'd spent months imagining his arms around her, his body moving with hers.

Martin reached down and stripped off her shirt, unhooked her bra, and set about exploring her breasts with just as much curiosity as the first time.

"Hello ladies." He rested his cheek between them. "How I have missed you."

"Seriously?" Sunny bit her lip to keep from laughing.

"Shhh." He put his hands over both her breasts. "I can talk to you on the phone. I can't speak to them."

Sunny started to laugh and Martin laughed along with her. She scooted out of her leggings while he took off his shirt and wriggled out of his pants. They were demolishing the orderly pillows arranged on the bed, and neither of them seemed to care.

"I missed you," he said.

"I missed this." She was desperate for him. He

pressed his chest against her body and they were skin to skin. The contact was incandescent and the sun slanting through the windows cast striped shadows across their skin. She felt as if she would ignite if he didn't touch her.

Martin put his hand between her thighs and Sunny nearly came from the first touch. She was swollen with want, aching for him. He eased one finger inside her, then another. She twisted beneath him, pulling him closer as he teased her mercilessly.

The climax took her with the violence of a sudden wave. As she was coming around his fingers, he eased them from the grip of her body and slid himself inside in one smooth motion, encasing his erection within her and pausing when he'd filled her to the hilt.

She wrapped her arms around his shoulders and held him as the aftershocks of her climax shook her torso.

He pressed his forehead to hers. "I love you."

"I love you too."

Martin moved in her, and months of longing meant that his climax ambushed him as quickly as hers did. He let out a long breath, kissing her neck over and over as she lightly ran her nails up and down his back.

Everything about her felt effervescent. She was in

Nairobi with Martin. He loved her. She loved him. She was staying in Kenya and they were going to try.

"Please don't rent an apartment." He kissed along her jaw. "Stay here. Stay with me. I don't want to be without you again. I was... not a very pleasant person to be around when I thought I'd lost you."

"Yes, Alice might have mentioned that."

Martin's body shook with laughter. "Errol said I was grumpier than a buffalo. When you come back to the Mara, the employees will likely give you a standing ovation for taking me back."

"You can't have been that bad." She kissed his jaw. "I like the beard. It's really handsome."

"Thank you. My father told me to shave it off and go to the States to work things out with you if I was going to be so moody."

She looked at him. "Really?"

"Really." He smiled again. "Please stay with me, my Sunny. I promise I won't be a grumpy buffalo."

She closed her eyes and reveled in the delicious weight of Martin's chest resting in the curve of her body. "I'll think about it." She was going to give in; she already knew it. He was too sweet and she was too happy. "Can you cook?"

"No, but I will hire a cook when we are in the city,

and I will bring you tea in bed every morning. Do we have a deal?"

"So businesslike."

"Yes." Martin bit her earlobe. "Do we have a deal, Miss Randolph?"

"Yes, Mr. Karanja." She kissed him again. "We have a deal."

Epilogue

Almost two years later

SUNNY SAT in the passenger seat of the Land Cruiser, looking up from the PDF she was reading on her tablet as they watched the safari plane sweep around the airstrip, gradually getting lower and lower until the wheels bounced on the dirt track, kicking up dust as the plane approached the waiting vehicles.

"What birthday is this?"

"Eighty-nine." Martin turned to smile at her. "She's just humoring us now. Apparently she was hiking in the Simean Mountains in Ethiopia a week ago."

The Simean Mountains were over twelve-thousand

feet. "So a safari with us is her version of a relaxing beach vacation?"

"I'm afraid we're not challenging enough for Ethel anymore." Martin put the truck in gear and eased over toward the side of the plane where ground crew were already taking out luggage and guests in broad hats and sunglasses were climbing out of the plane.

It had been nearly two years since Sunny had joined Martin in Kenya, and only three months since they'd married in a quiet service at her parents' house in Chevy Chase. Martin's parents were planning the big society wedding for the following summer, but luckily her mother-in-law would take care of all those details, since the thought of planning a society wedding in Nairobi made Sunny hyperventilate.

"Do you think Ethel might want to come for the wedding?" she asked. "I mean, she was there at the beginning. She might want to be there for the big party too."

"Were you planning to have extreme sports at the reception?" Martin stared over the dashboard of the Land Cruiser, his eyes covered by dark wrap-around sunglasses. "Perhaps we could sky-dive into the park for our grand entrance? She might accompany us if we did that."

"I know." She reached for his hand and squeezed it.

"We could get married in mid-air, Ethel officiating the ceremony, and live-stream it to the guests below."

Martin stared at her in horror. "Who are you, and what have you done with my cautious wife?"

Sunny smiled, delighted to have horrified her usually unflappable husband. "I'm just saying, Ethel would be game for it."

"Please don't suggest it, because you're absolutely right."

Marrying Martin was the easiest choice that Sunny had ever made. They were so well-suited for each other, even her mother had been forced to admit that moving to Kenya had been a brilliant plan. In fact, Sunny was fairly certain her mother told her club friends that it had been Mitsy's idea in the first place.

"My parents wanted to come out in January." Sunny spotted Ethel in the distance, springing out of the plane as if she was a teenager. "Get out of the cold for a bit."

Martin shuddered. He'd experienced Washington winter and was not a fan. "That's understandable."

"Mom wanted to know if the Duma Tent was available."

Her parents, much to her surprise, had fallen in love with Kenya nearly as much as Sunny had. They'd flown out three times to visit, and were constantly telling their friends about their son-in-law's famous safari camp.

"Talk to Alice." Martin opened his door and hopped out. "I'm sure we can make it work. Most people don't have specific requests for tents like your mother."

She leaned over and smiled sweetly. "Thank you for loving my high-maintenance mother."

He laughed. "She's no more high maintenance than mine."

Martin's parents and Sunny's parents had met and almost immediately become friends. Her mother and her mother-in-law bonded over their love of charity boards, and her dad and Martin's father shared a passion for golf. The Karanjas had already visited Chevy Chase and Sunny was fairly certain they had plans to go back, with or without her and Martin.

Her phone buzzed with an email from a colleague in London who wanted to schedule a video chat for the following week. She typed out a reply and sent it back with a couple of times that she knew the connection at the camp would be good.

Moving to the continent of Africa had expanded her actuarial region, allowing her to consult with both the New York and the London branches of her bank. She still dreaded visiting the office, but twice a year in either place wasn't the worst development when most of her job could be done wherever she could get internet access.

Martin was walking back to the truck with Ethel beside him. He looked up and smiled at her, and Sunny's heart flipped over for the millionth time.

He was hers.

She was his, and he was hers and the life they were building was so beautiful, she got choked up when she thought about how she'd been living less than two years before.

She'd boarded a plane to Kenya, thinking she was going on a single adventure when the universe had so much more for her in store.

Adventure?

Love was the greatest adventure. And she couldn't wait to explore.

•◘•◘•◘•◘•

To learn more about Elizabeth Hunter's writing, please visit ElizabethHunterWrites.com or sign up for her newsletter!

Afterword

Dear Reader,

I don't often write contemporary romance, but when I went to Kenya in 2019, I was inspired by the landscape, the incredible beauty, and mostly the amazing people and safari team I met in the Mara.

Many readers know that my personal love story is an international one, so obviously many of the details about the challenges of international and cross-cultural relationships are drawn from my own experience. I do want to emphasize though, that Martin and Sunny's story is entirely fictional! This is not a retelling of my own love story. That might be a bit personal.

But in our travel and life internationally, my husband and I have made many friends for whom love started "worlds apart." Couples who—despite the challenges of geography, culture, and language—have built and continue to build rich lives and love stories together. This story is dedicated to them.

Thanks for reading, everyone. I appreciate all of you so much.

Elizabeth Hunter

Preview: The Genius and the Muse

Foothill Art Institute
Claremont, California
March 2010

Kate Mitchell tripped over the ridge of cracked asphalt, the stumble sending her backpack falling to the ground, scattering notebooks, pencils, and a bag of lens caps and filters across the parking lot. Her camera bag started to slide. She caught it just before the padded case slipped off her arm.

"Perfect," she said as she glared at the backpack. Kate shoved her unruly red hair out of her eyes and set the carefully packed camera case with her SLR and lenses to the side before she began to pick up the rest of the scattered mess from her backpack. She could already feel the sweat starting to trickle between her thin shoulder blades as the Southern California sun radiated from the blacktop. "As if this day couldn't get any better..."

She had a sneaking suspicion that she'd forgotten to put sunscreen on again, and she prayed her pale, freckled skin wouldn't be red by the time she got inside. She finished tossing the last of her school supplies in her backpack and hustled toward the old building set in the foothills of the San Bernardino Mountains.

As she neared the sprawling building that housed the school of visual arts, she heard the clanging and ringing of hammers from the metal-fabrication shop just past the ceramic kilns, and the chatter from a group of splattered painters who were gathered by a bench near the entrance. Kate finally reached the cool shade of a spreading pepper tree, set her bags down, and tried to tame her hair into a bun before continuing on toward her first class.

Though it wasn't even April, the temperatures were already expected to be in the high 80s, and Kate was flushed by the time she reached the glass doors of the entrance. She felt her phone vibrating in her pocket and grabbed it to read a message from her boyfriend.

Call me when you finish class and meetings today. —Cody

Curious, she sent back a quick text.

What's up? —Kate

Pulling open the side door to the building, she sighed at the rush of cool, dry air that poured out.

What are your plans this weekend?—C

She walked down the wide hall toward the restroom to check her hair, which had probably already flown in eight different directions.

I have thesis work, and there's an exhibition I need to go to.—K

No one else was in the bathroom, so Kate took a moment to splash water on her red, freckled face. She patted her skin dry, pulled herself together, and hurried out, checking the screen on her phone to see if she had enough time to make a quick pass through the alumni gallery before her History of Photography class.

Deciding she could stop for ten minutes, Kate turned right instead of left and wandered down the long hall containing past student work from notable alumni of Foothill Art Institute.

Nope. You're going to San Diego with me and the guys.—C

She rolled her eyes.

That's news to me.—K

Kate walked through the gallery, scanning the walls for any new additions. Her work would be here one day. She'd already picked out the print she would submit to her advisor, Professor Bradley. She may not have been sure of other parts of her life, but when it came to photography, Kate knew exactly where she wanted to go.

Come on, babe. Take a break for once. Mom already booked a room for you.—C

"Damn it, Cody, some of us don't run surf shops," she said to her phone. She thought about Cody's mom and dad, whom she had loved since she was a little girl. The last thing she wanted to do was ruin a weekend that Barbara had planned. Their families had been close friends for years. Their mothers met when Kate and Cody were babies. They'd grown up together, and had been friends before they developed an undeniable chemistry together as teenagers. By the time college rolled around, it took no one by surprise when they started dating.

Cody had been her first boyfriend and the only man she'd seriously dated since graduating from high school. In the back of her mind, she knew their parents were both expecting marriage. But Kate had always been focused on her education and her photography, and no one seemed to question whether she was settling too quickly.

Until recently, she hadn't questioned it herself.

She glared at her phone and sent a quick text back.

I can't. I've got to get this done, Cody. I've got deadlines coming up.—K

Cody had been supportive and proud of her work as long as they'd been together. He'd been her unofficial assistant on a shoot more than once, especially if it was at the beach. Still, the closer she got to finishing her master's thesis and getting serious about developing her portfolio, the more Cody seemed to be dissatisfied with where she was headed.

Walking swiftly past the screen prints and paintings at the beginning of the gallery, Kate moved around the partitions to make her way to the back corner where photography prints from past students hung scattered on the walls.

She felt her phone buzz again.

Fine. Whatever. I guess I'll tell my mom you're not coming. Maybe Brad can invite his girlfriend.—C

Shaking her head, Kate continued on toward the center of the photography exhibit. She stopped and sat on the small bench, trying to quash her irritation with Cody so she could absorb the numerous images produced by Foothill Art Institute's most famous graduate, Reed O'Connor. With her back to the rest of the gallery, she studied the early work of one of her favorite photographers, who was also partly the subject of her graduate project.

Reed O'Connor had made his name quickly in the art world. Still in his early thirties, his dramatic good looks, mysterious personal life, and reclusive persona made him an intriguing and attractive subject for gossip. But his work, in Kate's opinion, was the real mystery.

Even as a student, the tell-tale characteristics of what would come to be known as an "O'Connor portrait" were evident. Along with an impressive technical prowess, the young photographer exhibited an almost impressionistic use of light and shadow and an artful isolation of features. It was a singular style he'd perfected in the eight years since he graduated from Foothill.

Kate leaned her thin arms against the back of the bench and scanned the collection of photographs.

O'Connor's portrait work was often controversial to the celebrities and other public figures who clamored for his attention, but the artist had managed to create a stunning mystique with his meteoric rise from fashion to portrait photography. His portrait work had appeared in leading magazines around the world. He was notoriously private, constantly in demand, and stubbornly single-minded. He used no assistants, she knew from her research, and he absolutely *never* captured the subject's full visage.

"Hey, Kate? Are you in here?"

She turned, hearing a familiar voice call from the entrance of the gallery. She smiled when Michelle, her friend and roommate from freshman year, walked around a corner. Kate lifted a hand in greeting.

"Hey." She scooted over to share the small bench. "How'd you know I was in here?"

"Where else are you before your first class on Thursday?" Michelle sat down beside her. "Still studying the enigmatic portrait?"

"Mmhmm," Kate said with a nod; then both girls fell silent as they stared toward the wall. "It's just so... not him."

"But it is him."

"But it's not."

Michelle huffed. "Whatever, photography geek. You're obsessed."

The picture that continued to fascinate Kate, even after years of contemplation, was a small 8x10 in the top right corner of the wall. It wasn't a typical "O'Connor portrait" for a number of reasons—

though it might appear to be to someone less well-versed in his work. It had always caught her eye, despite the fact that it wasn't the most prominently displayed picture on the wall.

The light was unique. The lens, less sharply focused. Most importantly, instead of a singular focus for the camera's eye, the model was shown as if the photographer was looking over her right shoulder, and a man's hand was visible resting on it, as if he was trying to capture the girl or get her attention.

It was in soft black and white. The light spilled over the gentle curve of the girl's jaw, shadowing her neck and reflecting off the soft strands of hair, which waved behind her ear. Her head tilted as if the photographer had captured the image just before the subject turned her head, and the rise of the cheek hinted at a smile without showing one.

The man's hand rested on the shoulder, but the tips of the fingers curled, as if they were just about to grab hold. They were long and stained at the tips. Dark hair dusted the back of the hand and wrist. The nails were neat, but the skin was cracked near the cuticles. She'd always wondered if O'Connor was the owner of the hand and who the model was whom he'd captured with such uncharacteristic tenderness.

"Don't you have class at nine?"

Kate shrugged, still staring at the print on the wall.

"Kate?"

"Yeah?"

"Class, Kate." She felt Michelle shove her shoulder. "You know... the reason you've been coming here every day for six years?"

Finally, she shook her head and looked over at Michelle. "Yeah... class. What time is it?"

"About ten till. You should get going."

She grumbled and bent to pick up her backpack and camera bag. Tossing another look at the mystery portrait and hoisting her bags over her shoulder, she trudged toward the exit with Michelle.

"Hey!" Kate suddenly stopped, looking at her friend. "What are you doing in here? You don't have class on this floor, do you?"

"Oh!" Michelle's eyes lit up. "Professor Seever told me about some new sketches that someone cleaning out the painting studio found last month. They're by Rhodes, from when she was going here. Just anatomy studies, I guess, but she's notable enough now that they matted them and put them up. I was going to take a look."

Kate nodded toward the painting section. "Well, let's go. My class is right down the hall, so I still have a few minutes. Plus"—she grinned— "Bradley's teaching this one; he won't mind if I'm a little late."

"A little?" Michelle laughed. Heading toward the opposite side of the long, narrow gallery, the two girls approached a collection of paintings from various graduates, some still known and many others who had drifted into obscurity. In the middle of the far wall, between an abstract portrait in charcoal and a watercolor seascape in oils, hung three simple frames containing pen and ink studies. They were small, no more than eight by twelve inches, but had been matted so the notable signature of the artist was evident.

S. Rhodes.

The top sketch was a study of a man's arm and neck from the side. It was long and muscled, the definition particularly detailed along the neck and shoulder. The middle picture was a leg and foot. The thigh was lean and defined, its knee bent as if the model was lying down on a flat surface.

It was when Kate's eyes reached the bottom sketch that her breath caught in her throat. She stepped closer, her eyes riveted to the wall. Inside the plain matte was the study of a male hand—a very familiar hand. In fact, one glance told her that the long fingers, smooth calluses and slightly cracked cuticles of that hand belonged, without a doubt in her mind, to the same man who grasped the shoulder of the model in the mysterious O'Connor portrait.

She stared, transfixed by the same hand that she had studied from a different angle, in a unique work, done in an entirely separate medium on the other side of the gallery.

"Kate?"

"It's the same," she whispered. "It has to be. Who—"

"Kaitlyn?"

Her wide blue eyes finally left the frame to stare blankly at her friend.

"Huh?"

Michelle looked at her watch. "Class, Kate. You're going to be *really* late if you don't leave right now."

"Oh." She drew in a ragged breath. "Okay, thanks."

Michelle cocked her head and looked at her. "You all right?"

Kate nodded. "Uh-huh. Sure. We, uh... we better go."

Glancing back at the sketch, Kate turned and left the alumni gallery where the two hands, one drawn in pen and one captured by the lens, almost seemed to reach toward each other from opposite silent walls.

•◘•◘•◘•◘•

THE GENIUS AND THE MUSE is a standalone romance available in ebook, paperback, and audio from all major retailers.
ElizabethHunter.com

Looking for more?

Whether you're a fan of romance, contemporary fantasy, fantasy romance, or paranormal women's fiction, Elizabeth Hunter has a series for you.

Love Stories on 7th and Main

Small town romance with heart and humor! Fall into a friendly crowd of artists, bakers, booksellers, and friends who are starting fresh, finding love, and building new lives together. Things heat up on Main Street when Emmie Elliot moves back to revive her grandmother's bookshop. Staying in her hometown was never the plan, but when you visit Metlin, it's hard not to feel at home.

Ebook/Audiobook/Paperback

THE ELEMENTAL MYSTERIES

Discover the series that has millions of vampire fans raving! Immortal book dealer Giovanni Vecchio thought he'd left the bloody world of vampire politics behind when he retired as an assassin, but a chance meeting at a university pulls student librarian Beatrice De Novo into his orbit. Now temptation lurks behind every dark corner as Vecchio's growing attachment to Beatrice competes with a series of clues that could lead to a library lost in time, and a powerful secret that could reshape the immortal world.

Ebook/Audiobook/Paperback/Hardcover

THE CAMBIO SPRINGS MYSTERIES

Welcome to the desert town of Cambio Springs where the water is cool, the summers sizzle, and all the residents wear fur, feathers, or snakeskin on full moon nights. In a world of cookie-cutter shifter romance, discover a series that has reviewers raving. Five friends find themselves at a crossroads in life; will the tangled ties of community and shared secrets be their salvation or their end?

Ebook/Audiobook/Paperback

THE IRIN CHRONICLES

"A brilliant and addictive romantic fantasy series." Hidden at the crossroads of the world, an ancient race battles to protect humanity, even as it dies from within. A photojournalist tumbles into a world of supernatural guardians protecting humanity from the predatory sons of fallen angels, but will Ava and Malachi's attraction to each other be their salvation or their undoing?

Ebook/Audiobook/Paperback

GLIMMER LAKE

Delightfully different paranormal women's fiction! Robin, Val, and Monica were average forty-something moms when a sudden accident leaves all three of them with psychic abilities they never could have predicted! Now all three are seeing things that belong in a fantasy novel, not their small mountain town. Ghosts, visions, omens of doom. These friends need to stick together if they're going to solve the mystery at the heart of Glimmer Lake.

Ebook/Audiobook/Paperback

And there's more! Please visit ElizabethHunter.com or sign up for her newsletter to read more about her work.

About the Author

ELIZABETH HUNTER is an eleven-time *USA Today* and international best-selling author of romance, contemporary fantasy, and paranormal mystery. Based in Central California and Addis Ababa, she travels extensively to write fantasy fiction exploring world mythologies, history, and the universal bonds of love, friendship, and family.

She has published over fifty works of fiction. She is the author of the Glimmer Lake series, Love Stories on 7th and Main, the Elemental Legacy series, the Irin Chronicles, the Cambio Springs Mysteries, and other works of fiction.

Also by Elizabeth Hunter

Contemporary Romance

The Genius and the Muse

7th and Main

INK

HOOKED

GRIT

SWEET

Linx & Bogie Mysteries

A Ghost in the Glamour

A Bogie in the Boat

The Elemental Mysteries

(Giovanni and Beatrice)

A Hidden Fire

This Same Earth

The Force of Wind

A Fall of Water

The Stars Afire

Fangs, Frost, and Folios

The Elemental World

(various characters)

Building From Ashes

Waterlocked (novella)

Blood and Sand

The Bronze Blade (novella)

The Scarlet Deep

Beneath a Waning Moon (novella)

A Stone-Kissed Sea

The Elemental Legacy

(Ben and Tenzin)

Shadows and Gold

Imitation and Alchemy

Omens and Artifacts

Midnight Labyrinth

Blood Apprentice

Night's Reckoning

Dawn Caravan

The Bone Scroll